D0953784

Praise for *What We Saw at Night*

AN AMERICAN BOOKSELLERS ASSOCIATION INDIE NEXT SELECTION

Nominated for:
YALSA BEST FICTION FOR YOUNG ADULTS AWARD
YALSA 2014 QUICK PICKS AWARD
THE SOUTH CAROLINA BOOK AWARD

"The plot is intricately woven, with twists at every turn . . . masterful."
—Karin Slaughter, *New York Times* bestselling author of *Criminal*

"Dangerously addictive, breathtakingly beautiful, terminally awesome."
—Lauren Myracle, *New York Times* bestselling author of *Shine*

"A thrilling ride . . . Dark, suspenseful and quietly beautiful."
—Melissa Walker, acclaimed author of *Small Town Sinners*

"*What We Saw at Night* is an engaging blend of real-world drama involving a life-and-death illness and a whodunit thriller. Imagine John Green's *The Fault in Our Stars* in a mash-up with a Nancy Drew mystery. Plus some roof jumping and wall scaling."—*Pittsburgh Post-Gazette*

"Allie's voice is honest and real . . . fascinating looks at both Parkour and a disease so unconventional that it turns the lives of patients and families upside down."—*Booklist*, High Demand Review

"Atmospheric, melancholy . . . breathtaking."—*Publishers Weekly*

"The fast pace is set from the beginning with Juliet's dazzling jump across the buildings . . . recommended for readers who enjoy a unique twist on realistic fiction."—*VOYA Magazine*

"This latest from Mitchard is quickly paced and intricately plotted, with flares of humor cobbled into the dialogue . . . The suspense will keep [readers] engrossed."—*Kirkus Reviews*

"A page-turner . . . the cliff-hanger ending will have readers waiting for the next installment."—*School Library Journal*

Also by Jacquelyn Mitchard

What We Saw at Night

WHAT
WE
LOST
IN THE
DARK

JACQUELYN MITCHARD

Published in the United States in 2013 by Soho Teen
an imprint of Soho Press, Inc.
853 Broadway
New York, NY 10003

Library of Congress Cataloging-in-Publication Data

Mitchard, Jacquelyn.
What we lost in the dark / by Jacquelyn Mitchard.
p. cm
ISBN 978-1-61695-143-6
eISBN 978-1-61695-144-3
1. Xeroderma pigmentosum—Fiction. 2. Serial murderers—Fiction.
3. Survival—Fiction. 4. Racially mixed people—Fiction
5. Family life—Minnesota—Fiction. 6. Scuba diving—Fiction.
7. Superior, Lake—Fiction. 8. Minnesota—Fiction. I. Title.
PZ7.M6848Wg 2013
[Fic]—dc23 2013016762

Interior design by Janine Agro, Soho Press, Inc.
Interior art by Michael Fusco

Printed in the United States of America

10 9 8 7 6 5 4 3 2 1

For Karin Slaughter

"Be not the slave of your own past. Dive deep and swim far, so you shall come back with self-respect, with new power ... that shall explain and overlook the old."
—RALPH WALDO EMERSON

to be tacked on for tourists—although tourists flock to Iron Harbor for reasons I've never been quite able to fathom. At the center stands a monument to Amos Hayden of the Union's First Minnesota Infantry regiment, another ghost, sweet and sad. The town's Civil War hero, he was a miner's son. At Gettysburg, when nothing except a doomed charge with fixed bayonets could hold back the rebels, the general turned to the First Minnesota, the soldiers who were closest to him. Two hundred and sixty-two men charged, and two hundred and fifteen died. Not a single man deserted. It was over in fifteen minutes. They gave their lives for an idea that not all of them probably even understood.

Amos Hayden was only seventeen. His statue is here, but he still sleeps in that ground so far away.

Was he brave or only young?

Did he have a moment to think of his mother? Or the lakeshore where he skipped stones, or the summer stars so close you felt you could reach up and play with them like beads? Did a girl love him and wait for him to come back to her? Did he know that he might never again open the door on an icy wind that slapped him to run?

Tonight, nobody is thinking of Amos Hayden dying young and alone. It's late fall, and people visiting this town are taking advantage of the warmth of an extended autumn. They stroll past the Flying Fish restaurant and Borealis Books, with its neat scalloped wooden fringes—each painted to resemble a famous volume of prose. Even the tall pale girl with the uncombed auburn hair, who stops in front of the statue and stares . . . the tall pale girl who is me . . . even she isn't really thinking of Amos Hayden, although I remember looking up into his earnest and good-natured face, the face that would always be young.

Only later, when I passed the scene of the place where I had the only true mental meltdown I would ever have in my life, did I stop to consider Amos Hayden. I wondered then, how could the most innocent of heroes and the pond scum of sinners rise from this one small place? Iron Harbor is very small indeed, four hundred people, four thousand in summer. Twenty streets.

That Sunday night was only a few weeks after my best friend's murdered body was found.

If she were here, Juliet would not be an ordinary ghost. She would be an angry ghost, punishing and malign. I was angry, too.

So that night I walked into one of the two clothing stores, and I stole a poncho.

I had never stolen so much as a pack of gum.

If all the boutiques in Beverly Hills had opened, all at once for my own personal plunder, and I could run through them and keep whatever I wanted—until my arms and shopping carts were filled—I would sooner have chosen a rhinestone cat collar than a poncho. And I don't even have a cat.

The one I pulled down was woven in shades of green, from mint to forest—a thick, subtly striped garment with the kind of oily, expensive feeling that seems to scoff at all weather. Ladies from Chicago bought these to wear on their sailboats. The store was a typical wannabe Native American thread-and-head shop that is required on the map of every tourist town.

I slipped the thing on.

Then I walked out the door.

The owner, an old bearded hippie guy everybody called Corona, watched me curiously. He didn't say a word.

Corona's store was one of the few places that Juliet and

Rob and I had never been able to break into. Corona was in the gifted program for theft prevention.

I call it "breaking in," but we never broke a thing.

We were way too good for that. We left things just as they were, or a little tidier. Juliet could be light-fingered when it came to expensive wine and trinkets, but Rob and I kept her in check. She was the first one to get a set of lock picks (you can buy them online), and we all quickly followed her lead. The *tres compadres*, we roamed the night, from fancy, faux Swiss ski chalets in the hills where we sipped champagne in the owners' hot tubs to the music store where we pounded our palms on drums or ran our fingers over the electric guitar strings, me playing the only chords I knew, the opening riff to "Smoke on the Water."

We owned Iron Harbor, Minnesota.

It was ours.

Really, though, Iron Harbor, and our place in it, in its night landscape, was mostly Juliet's. Juliet was always at the wheel, no matter who was really driving. Rob and I rode shotgun to her desire.

Her chief desire?

That was to be free—not free of us, her closest friends on earth, but of this place and of her life in it.

Now she was free, forever, of the former and the latter.

Wearing the poncho like a flag, I reached the end of the street. Then I stopped and burst into tears. It was a warm night, sixty-eight degrees at nine o'clock. It's never this warm, this late in the year, so far north.

Corona had joined me at the corner. He was a tall old guy, thin to the point of gauntness, with a face I now noticed was lined not with the wrinkles of care, but with decades of quiet amusement. His eyes brimmed with a surpassing kindness.

Why had we ever tried to burgle his little place? As we gazed at each other, I saw that he knew that we had tried, and it was already forgiven.

"It's okay, little dude," he said.

Corona took the phone out of my hand and scrolled down until he found the favorite labeled *Mom*.

She was there within five minutes, jumping out of the mini-van, leaving the driver's side door hanging open in the middle of the intersection. I might as well have been a toddler, for the way my mother held up my arms and slipped the poncho over my head. Then, she stroked my hair. "Oh, Allie . . . oh, Allie."

"I stole this from him," I confessed. My teeth started to chatter.

Corona just shrugged. "It's okay. I don't care if she keeps it, even."

Everyone knew about Juliet. Everyone knew I was crazy.

"I *stole* this!" I repeated, raising my voice.

Corona gave my mother a level look.

Mom sighed. "Allie," she said. "Honey. Time to go home."

"Why don't you call the cops?" I glared at her, and then at Corona. "Call Tommy. Call Mr. Sirocco. No, don't call him. But call someone." Juliet's father, Tommy Sirocco, was the chief of the Iron County Sheriff's Department, and deeply in mourning for his only child. "Doesn't anybody around here ever do anything? Doesn't anyone care when someone does something wrong?"

"You aren't a bad person. You didn't do anything wrong, tonight or ever. You couldn't have helped her, Allie," Mom said, pulling me close. I shook my head, squeezing my eyes shut and struggling against my mother, now really acting like a toddler, literally kicking at her shins with the toes

with someone who could provide forensic voiceprints. But Dr. Yashida believed me. I might seem like a crazy to the Iron County cops, but I had good reasons for someone outside this strange protectorate to believe me.

I tried to think of all the good now that would come from my soon-to-begin future.

I tried to think of having a future. All I could think of was Juliet, and how she had lain, exposed and broken, in the very building where I would be working. I knew from reading that the pursuit of criminals is always personal.

It shouldn't be that personal.

Mom said, "We went over this. The hands-on work will be invaluable. It's a good résumé item." One hand still on my arm, my mother piloted the car around the corner to our street. "The days will go past so quickly. This time will always be a terrible memory. But it's almost over now. Allie? Do you hear me?"

"I hear you," I said.

"Okay, then," said my mother.

"What if he's there?"

"You know he's not there! No one in that family is there. Every one of them except Dr. Andrew's son Tim is in Bolivia. You *know* that, Allie. You saw that on the news. You saw them leaving." My mother stopped the car in our driveway. "You got a letter from the night supervisor about your volunteer service . . ."

I snorted. In my mind, Garrett Tabor could be anywhere he wanted to be. My fear had assumed the proportions of reverence, invested him with the superpowers.

"Well, you did. You saw them leave. On that note, Dr. Stephen said he regretted that he wouldn't be around to help you, and that he hoped you had a good experience."

This was also true. Even though the general belief was that I'd tried to boil his boy alive, Dr. Stephen Tabor seemed genuinely concerned for me—and even enthused.

"Do you believe that?" my mother said.

"I believe you."

At least one of us should relax. I didn't believe her, at all.

"I believe you," Angie said. Then, I had to smile.

"No one will punish you anymore. It's over," Mom added.

On both counts, she was wrong.

A week later, when I showed up for my community service, the first person I saw was Garrett Tabor, the man who murdered Juliet, and who knows how many other girls, and who also would murder me.

THE FIRST TIME

2

ONCE AGAIN, FOR THE FIRST TIME

The night I arrived at the lab, I pulled into the parking lot, then nearly jerked the wheel of the car around and went home.

There was the little red Italian sports car—the car that had twice almost run me down, the car that Garrett Tabor drove.

But that was silly.

What had Mom said? None of the Tabors was around. I breathed out, as a therapist taught me after my best friend's strange death. "Breathe out, breathe out," she said. "The body would always breathe in on its own." I listened for my heartbeat to obey, following the meter of my breathing down and down.

It wasn't Garrett Tabor. The car belonged to his pathologist father, Dr. Stephen.

Why it was parked here, instead of in Steve's garage? I had no idea. He could park his car anywhere he wanted.

I stood up straighter and pressed the button on the

steel door. A buzz prompted me to enter the one-story concrete-block building that housed the Iron County Medical Examiner's Office. When I got inside, though, there was no one in the short hall that separated the lab and morgue from the offices.

"Hello?" I said. "Hello?"

The interim night supervisor would be a medical doctor, or a nurse practitioner like my mother. There would also be an evidence technician to train me.

From behind me, I heard a sudden clicking and slithering, like a snake wearing cleats.

"Good evening, Allie," said Garrett Tabor. "How are you?"

I whirled like a child's top. A whimper escaped my throat. I saw the pleasure rippling across his face. Not in Bolivia, he stood two feet from me. *Blondie*. It was the streak of platinum that ran down the wavy dark pelt of his hair. The first time I saw that streak, Tabor was hunched over a half-naked girl in an empty apartment.

Garrett Tabor: trusted ski coach, privileged son, genetic researcher, and serial killer.

Does that surprise you?

Does it surprise you that a serial killer was walking around?

The great majority of them are walking around. The great majority look like everyone else. My criminology books call them "unsubs," meaning that they're unknown. Some even look a little better than most—unless you catch the unguarded flat gaze of the predator, sympathetic as a grizzly. They present a front that's civil, even charming. That's how they get people.

I put my hand behind me on the door handle. It didn't budge.

Tabor shrugged. "It's a government office. It has to be locked at night. There's a code you punch in on that pad."

A code.

"That's illegal," I said. "What if there was a fire?"

Or a murder?

"Of course there are emergency exits."

I wouldn't be able to find them. The over-breathing rose like floodwater. You can have one panic attack or you can have fifty; and they all feel like you're dying. I rummaged in my front pack for my keys, tethered to my phone case.

"Let me out," I said finally, gasping.

"You can leave whenever you want," Garrett Tabor said.

"Where's the supervisor?"

Garrett Tabor shrugged again. "Nobody's here but us."

Shit. Shit. Shit. A panic attack . . . incoming, incoming. I punched in button two, the one that led to my boyfriend, Rob Dorn. Answer, I prayed. Answer.

"I'm organizing my data from Bolivia," he said. "I came back early."

"I'll call the police."

I could hear Rob, distantly saying, "Allie? Hello? Allie?" I pressed the speaker. "I'm right here," I said. "I'm in the lab with Garrett Tabor. So you know." To Tabor, I said again, "I'm going to call the police."

"To say what?" Tabor said. As always, he was right. "I just want a chance to tell you I feel badly about this, Allie."

"Badly?"

"This is all so sad. First Juliet. Then this thing with you. So much hurt could have been avoided. I realize how impaired your judgment was. I'll give you that much." He smiled, a dog's grin, avid and yet patient. "I'm trying to move past this."

"Move past it . . . ? You're crazy," I said. "Let me out."
I almost added *please*. I was sweating and lunging like a runner who'd left everything on the track. Tabor looked as at
ease in this house of the dead as he would have looked in
his own bedroom. Of course he did. Just as Dr. Stephen ran
this office, and Dr. Andrew Tabor ran the Tabor Clinic, they
owned the condominiums, the ski and dive rentals, the motor
lodges, and two of the restaurants. Iron Harbor was the name
of this place only by virtue of geography. It should be called
Tabor-ville.

I stared now at the scion of that great family of healers.

That I was even here was because Garrett Tabor's lies
were better than my truth. After Juliet's death, he said I had
scaled the balconies to his apartment—a place, of course,
called the Tabor Oaks Condominiums. He said I'd broken in
wearing a ski mask and poured boiling water on him as he
lay innocently in bed.

How could adults believe pure shit? I . . . poured boiling
water on him? I found the stove in a place I'd never been, and
put a teakettle on, with Tabor one wall away? If I'd gone to
the trouble to catch him vulnerable, why didn't I just bring a
big hammer and hit him with it? Still, Tabor had the surveillance tapes of Rob and Juliet and I climbing the outside walls
that long-ago night. He had second-degree burns rippling
along his neck and a ski mask I'd once owned.

WHAT WAS TRUE was that I was a gifted climber.

Rob and Juliet and I had practiced the urban discipline
called Parkour, and there was almost no place that we could
not boulder up or leap down from. We had indeed traced
the Tabor Oaks, and had seen Tabor there. Those tapes had
no time stamp. We were high with the triumph when I saw

him with that still, colorless, half-naked young woman whose name no one would probably ever know, helpless, her clothing and her dignity torn away, by those same immaculate hands.

I called the police back then.

I called them later, when Garrett Tabor forced me to jump from the third story of a parking garage, breaking my arm so badly I had to have surgery.

I called when he threatened me, and again when he cornered me in a local cemetery, finally chasing me all the way into town until I screamed for help front of Gitchee Pizza.

The owner, Gideon Brave Bear, a true friend and a true drunk, fired off both barrels of his shotgun. Gideon got a ticket. Tabor got the satisfaction of knowing that no one believed Gid or me. It was always my word against his. His word always prevailed.

Except once.

After Juliet's memorial service, when I got the phone calls, I didn't risk calling the police. The only person I trusted was Dr. Barry Yashida, my advisor at John Jay University. A man I'd met only once on Skype, he had kept my confidence, and kept what I gave him.

It wasn't even the horror of Juliet's disappearance, or the confirmation that Juliet's DNA matched the badly mauled remains pulled from the river three weeks later.

The phone calls diced my guts.

Deep in sedative-soaked sleep after Juliet's memorial, I never heard my phone go off. The following night, my breath stopped when I beheld the screen: five calls from Juliet's phone.

Dead for weeks, Juliet left me five pleading, chilling phone messages.

Dr. Yashida, who'd been FBI for thirty years, had the voiceprint of the phone call compared with the old videos Juliet and I made, of us dancing, or modeling the clothes we'd bought. At least three were a near-perfect match for her voice. CD copies of those calls were in the fireproof safe in Rob's ceiling.

Now I knew that those calls had been recorded long ago.

A heartless ruse from a soulless creature, they had done the job that they were meant to do on my head.

He wanted me to think there was slimmest chance that Juliet was still alive and needed me. If I told anyone, I would pull the trigger on the even-worse: if she were alive, then she would die because of me.

Since then, my mother and my sister and I lived not only with blackout shades on the windows but with motion sensors in the yard and, on the doors, thick, steel prison locks that opened only to a code we changed weekly. It made me strange. My little sister Angela had to text me twice to prove she was at school before I could sleep. I would check the door and window locks, not just once but twenty times. Next to my bed—along with my sleep mask, my Maglite, and my miner's headlamp, and the stack of journals I'd been writing in since I was twelve—I now also kept the kind of weighted baseball bat that hitters use in practice, a gift Rob insisted on giving me, admittedly not the most romantic token you could imagine, but protective. Rob's dad had a collection of a couple of hundred of those bats that once belonged to sluggers in the pros. He gave them like golden tickets to the owners of sporting goods stores who were good boys and girls and pushed lots of gear with official team logos—the stuff Mr. Dorn sold. We figured he wouldn't miss one.

A bat like that could kill with one swing.

NOW, HERE I was, in a morgue, in the approximate dead center of nowhere, filled with silence and saws and poisons, facing the man who bequeathed such madness.

The police had come to think of me as an overheated sick girl with an overactive imagination and a grudge against the family to whom I literally owed my life.

If you went even further back, I was here not only because of what Garrett Tabor was, but because of what I was.

I wouldn't have been trapped in this pus-green hallway with a murderous sicko if my parents didn't fall for someone with a recessive gene that turned out to be well . . . me. I was born with Xeroderma Pigmentosum, or XP, the deadly "allergy" to sunlight. So was Juliet, and so was Rob. So if I were the best singer who ever lived, I could never be on Broadway. The spotlights would fry me to a crisp. If you have XP, you are the bread, and life is the toaster.

A boy once dismissed Juliet by saying she was pretty hot for a girl who had to go home every morning and sleep in her coffin. Well, we weren't dead, or even undead, but we only came out at night, or, on rare occasions, in daylight, wearing light-resistant regalia that made us look like we were going to battle against the Imperial forces without benefit of atmosphere. The only line of defense between XP and me was the Tabor Clinic, the world's eminent research and treatment facility.

Garrett Tabor's grandfather, Simon, founded the Tabor Clinic.

With Simon's own sons following in his footsteps, Dr. Andrew treated the living. Garrett Tabor's father, Stephen, a pathologist, analyzed the tissues of those who died from XP, along with his duties as ME.

When it came to this disease, they were the top researchers on earth.

So why wasn't the Tabor Clinic in New York or San Diego, but instead here, in the northernmost northwoods, on the edge of a village that made Paris, Illinois, look like Paris, France?

It was for a prosaic reason. Dr. Simon liked to ski. His family had a cottage in Iron Harbor when he was a boy, and he brought his own young family here from the University of Chicago. Dr. Simon's now several hundred years old, but he still skis. Watching him water-ski is like seeing one of those movies in which the skeletons in armor spring up from dragon's teeth.

From all over the world, the Tabor Clinic attracted families like Rob's, Allie's, and mine. Some of them had younger kids with the telltale clusters of big, dark freckles that often characterize the disease. There were older XP patients in Iron Harbor, but not much older. There were even other teenagers, but the hide-inside kind. For the three of us, sunset was the dawn. We rushed out into a bright new night, to find something to do—or simply to raise some hell.

We'd grown up inseparable, as loyal as you can be only to someone who saw you eat sand and then skinny dip, who saw you hide your first lost tooth under your pillow in a bag tied with a ribbon and then hide your beer under the pier in a bag tied with a clothesline.

It felt like forever sometimes.

And then Juliet changed. It was nearly imperceptible at first. She was always different when she was skiing, so it seemed like any other year. Juliet was one of Tabor's ski prodigies—a gifted aerialist and at practically no risk to her at all (except the obvious risks of flipping around a hundred and fifty feet in the air down a hill). Because XP people have very weak eyes, she wore specially treated glasses. All the rest of her, every inch, by the very nature of the sport, was covered, slick as a sexy seal in Juliet's trademark midnight blue. By the time she was fourteen, she was nationally ranked, known for the deceptively reckless grace of her spins and flips.

Then, so quietly at first we never sensed a thing, Tabor began to spin into Juliet's life, to spin his web.

Tabor used my Juliet's lust for freedom to push her past skiing, making her his live doll, his sexual toy—when she was not yet fifteen.

Still, even then, when Tabor had her in his coils, "us" still meant the three of us. Even after last year, when Rob realized that he was as much in love with me as I had been with him since I was eleven, which should have ended it, we were the *tres compadres*. The primary "us" was the first "us" that existed—Juliet and me. Rob and me. Juliet and Rob and me.

Only death parted us.

We could have died from Parkour, but if you're going to die young, and we probably were, you crave thrills. While Juliet was a skier, Rob and I would crawl into caves so narrow that Rob's broad shoulders barely fit—caves that could have been home to rabid wolverines—just to do it. On our own skis, we went not down cliffs, but off the edges. Then Juliet took a bad fall, and doctors learned that her vision had deteriorated so much that she had the eyesight of a vole. She was through. She almost lost her mind.

Break-ins and brewfests kept us going for a while. But then, just in time, before we turned to vices in a get-busted way, Juliet led us to Parkour. Every dull structure in our very dull town became something to vault, to conquer. We got bruises and blisters, big biceps, concussions, and broken bones. We violated people's privacy and we trespassed—on private and government property. And it was all ferociously magical until we scaled the Tabor Oaks, where we saw what crawled out at night.

3

THROWDOWN

"If you want to stay, my father left your instructions on that empty desk over there," Garrett Tabor said.

"I'm not staying," I said. "Screw that."

I could feel my guts constrict, like wet laundry. After Juliet, life for me was holding its breath. Would I let him make me go on holding my breath forever?

"Allie, Allie, don't look so scared," Tabor said. "I'm not the big bad wolf."

"That's insulting to wolves," I said quietly. I breathed in, normally. "You should be scared. Someone is going to get you."

"Somebody already tried. You."

"You know that's a lie," I said. I thought of Juliet, silhouetted against the sky, arms and skis joyously outstretched. The year she had to stop was the first time that girls could compete at the Olympic level in the ski jump; Juliet could have been a pioneer. It didn't seem possible, but at that moment, I hated Tabor even more. "Juliet wasn't afraid of you."

"I don't know. Do you know? Who knows her better? Me? Or you?"

"No one knows her like I do," I said.

"You knew her as a childhood friend," he said. "I was her friend when she was a young woman."

"You were her rapist."

Tabor's charm slid off his face like snow off the hood of a hot car. Beneath the mask there was nothing. His face was the front of a locked building. He said, "You know that isn't true."

"I know it is," I said. "So did Juliet. So does my mother. Does your mother know?"

With a visible gathering, Tabor rebuilt his countenance. He smiled like a stroke victim, just relearning how.

"My mother's dead," Garrett Tabor said, his pleasant gaze unwavering. "She died in a car accident, on Christmas Eve. With her baby daughter." Reflex almost prompted me to offer a condolence. I didn't, though. He might not even have been telling the truth. He went on, "I know you don't really put a lot of faith in my friendship with Juliet. But it was very real. You know, the last time I saw Juliet was right here. That beautiful girl, stretched out on a stainless steel table . . . but you don't want to know about that."

My stomach began to boil. I thought of her the way they had found her, her teeth knocked out, her skin shredded, her lips ravaged by scuttling little crabs.

"You were here for Juliet's . . . autopsy?" The word was straightforward. It was a word I would have to get used to in my major.

"I wasn't here for that purpose," he said. "But I was in the building, yes. Are you sure you want to know about it?

"Not how you tell it. But the dead do speak to the living. Not by *leaving phone messages . . .*"

Did he blink?

He did. He flinched. No one else might have noticed it. But I did.

I dug in. "The dead speak. They tell you how they died by what they leave behind. If anybody ever stops people like you, it's going to be with evidence."

"Evidence is what landed you right here, Allie, I'm sad to say."

"That ski mask was Juliet's. It was mine once. But we switched ski masks. Hers was plain. She wanted the one my grandma sewed with fake rhinestones. She liked bling. But you know that."

"I know that. I know all that, Allie. I know just what Juliet liked."

Had he actually forgotten himself for a moment? My heart leapt. For a split second I rejoiced, wanting to do a little entrechat with a victory fist in the air. Garrett Tabor would keep on talking. And this dumpy place, after all, was more than a research lab or a morgue; it was an official government office. Everything would be on videotape. Garrett Tabor was putting the noose around his own neck. I had a short fantasy in which I presented my professor and advisor, Dr. Barry Yashida, with those tapes—skipping neatly around the roughnecks in what I thought about later being able to bring that proof to Juliet's father. But not now. Now, I would bide my time.

"I have work to do," I said.

"Yes, like putting death certificates in envelopes and sweeping the floor? Better get to it! We're both serving our community tonight, me as a healer and you as a . . . little drone."

"Maybe," I began. I took a deep breath. "Maybe it's

good I'm here. Maybe I can keep an eye on you. Did you ever think of that?"

Garrett Tabor turned away and shrugged in his white lab coat. "I think of everything, Allie."

Tears stabbed the backs of my eyes. "You . . . you pig," I said.

"Oh, don't be nasty. You're not supposed to talk trash to your superiors."

"I don't see anyone like that here. You're not superior. You're just old."

"And yet I'll last longer, Allie. I'll be going strong when you're just like Juliet."

"We'll see. We'll see who has the last word."

He turned back and nodded toward the surveillance camera, perched above the door. "Well, all these words would look bad if they were being recorded. But the little video cameras don't work. I think they're just for show. They've never worked. You know our hometown. Everything's a little down market in Iron Harbor. So, like I said. It's just you and me—"

"And me," said a mild voice.

A blast of cold air announced the arrival of my doctor, Bonnie Sommers Olsen. Not my XP doctor: that was Dr. Stephen's brother and Garrett's uncle, Andrew Tabor. Rather, my doctor for what little regular life I had.

"I'm here, too." Bonnie put her coat on the hook. The heavy steel door swung shut behind her. "The weather snapped. Cold out," she added. "Did you notice it was starting to snow?"

The night was filled with surprises. And yet, at that moment, I couldn't have been happier to see her if she'd jumped out of from behind a desk wearing a superhero cape.

"Why are you here?" I asked.

"Filling in," she said. "I'm subbing in as the supervisor while Dr. Stephen's gone, and I'll be working here a few nights a week on and off. Chris is at Northwestern. I'll be paying his tuition with my life insurance."

I loved Bonnie, even though she was a Daytimer—our term for people who lived on the regular clock instead of getting up when the sun went down. She was one of the few doctors on earth who didn't try to tell me, a chronically sick kid, to "go easy" or "be careful." Most important of all, Bonnie knew just what I thought about Garrett Tabor. She agreed with me that he was someone who made your skin crawl. Like my mother, she also knew that he'd slept with half the women at the hospital. None of that, however, proved that he was a killer.

But I would, I silently promised Juliet. I would do that on my own or die trying.

"Bonnie!" said Garrett Tabor with a big phony smile. "I should have known my dad wouldn't trust his lab to anyone but the best."

"Thank you, Garrett," Bonnie said evenly. "I think he trusted it to someone he knew would stay awake, because my blood is half caffeine by now."

"Bonnie, I happen to know you were an assistant medical examiner in Cook County, before you moved here," Garrett Tabor said. "Not a job many women would cherish. Women are all about healing."

"Knowing why people die is all about healing," Bonnie answered softly. "Hi, Allie. Have we got any guests tonight?"

Guests.

"Not quite a full house, but yes," said Garrett Tabor.

They meant bodies in the refrigerated drawers. Rubbing her hands along the arms of her long-sleeved sweatshirt,

Bonnie consulted a chalkboard list. "Oh no. Alex Trayhern. Of course. I knew that. That boy was in my son Elliott's class," she said. "Twelve years old. Hunting accident. And Vanessa Adams. A nurse. She was a good nurse, too . . . Who knows why people . . ."

"She was a suicide, correct?" Garrett Tabor said. "Injected herself with a syringe of air. She was about to be nailed for stealing prescription drugs, wasn't she? Don't nurses have the highest rates of suicide, Bonnie?"

"I'm sure you'd know better than I would, Garrett," she said. "You're a nurse."

"Well. You just ask me for whatever you need." He touched an imaginary hat brim.

"Perfect gentleman," Bonnie said, as he strolled away.

I told her, "That's what all the ladies say."

FEARS FOR TEARS

Time drained like a big hourglass with a fracture in the bottom, stoked by my fascination with all things terminal. The fascination, in turn, was stoked by my horrific recent past and my obsession with learning the truth about Juliet. The first time I looked up from filing reports about sudden or unusual deaths, my shift had ended.

It was already 1 A.M. The window thermometer showed that the temperature was just a few degrees above zero. I stifled a groan. For the past couple of weeks, the weather had seesawed this way, going late-summer warm in daytime, then skidding downward at night. I hadn't bothered with a heavy coat. But on my way out, Bonnie offered me an old parka that her younger son had left in the car that day. When I tried to refuse, she insisted.

"I know you'll return it. Besides, I know where you live," she joked.

I thanked her and bundled up.

✧ ✧ ✧ ✧ ✧

HURRYING OUT OF the medical examiner's building, I could think only of joining Rob in his huge and indecently comfortable bed, smack in the middle of his bachelor "apartment" over his family's garage. It was lucky that Rob's passion (besides me) involved computers, music mixing, and every kind of daredevil sport aside from raising elephants . . . or his parents would have turned the garage into a zoo.

Like every other XP parent except my mother, Rob's parents gave him everything. It made sense: Rob might not live to enjoy all the rewards of adulthood. The apartment his dad had made for him was to provide the illusion of independence. Although Rob would "go" to college online in the fall, he wouldn't really "go" anywhere. One of the agonies of a chronic illness is too much family togetherness. But my mother, convinced the research would beat XP before it beat me, saw no reason to give me anything more than a spare set of keys to her ancient Toyota minivan.

I was barely to the bottom step of the medical examiner's building when I heard the voice: low, urgent, infused with laughter.

"Allie," Garrett Tabor said into the frozen stillness. "Look what I have for you! A present."

I blinked at him in the frozen air. My pulse quickened. He held up my rhinestone-studded black ski mask. The one Juliet had "borrowed" in exchange for mine. The very key to how he'd framed me. But how had he gotten hold of it? "Don't you want this?" he asked. "All I want in return is a little forgiveness. A little compassion."

"That would require a little amnesia, don't you think?" I managed to say. "I'm going home."

Tabor took a step toward me. Something I couldn't really see glinted in his other hand, against the pale wool of a glove. A key? Or something more up Garrett Tabor's street? A scalpel? He wouldn't dare. I turned to head back in. Then I remembered. It was locked. It had to be locked. I had to buzz and hope Bonnie would set the land speed record for letting me in.

Or I had to act.

In Parkour, a tracer always "derives" a course. Although speed is key, no tracer ever goes forth without a plan. My heart punched in my chest. I could charge straight past Garrett Tabor, but once my back was to him, he would take me. People who run away in a straight line give their adversaries an advantage. Ask any soldier how to get caught, knocked down, or shot, and you'll get the same answer: *be predictable*. Parkour was created as a wartime discipline. Although I hadn't done it in months, the skills would not desert me.

Backing up, I took two steps and, placing both hands on the railing, swung my body straight up and over—my booted heels slicing the air near Tabor's head. He stepped back. I used that moment of disengagement to hit the panic button on my keys. The van erupted in horn blasts and flashing lights. Then I sprinted. I didn't breathe until I was swinging into the seat and peeling out of the lot, lightly kissing the immaculate tire of Tabor's red vintage sports car with the droopy bumper of our old Toyota.

I drove straight to Rob and didn't look back.

TEN MINUTES LATER, with the help of an elliptical machine and a straight-backed chair, I was reenacting my escape for Rob. Annoyingly calm, he lay on his back in the middle of his vast bed, smack in the middle of his "rooms." (This was Rob's classy term for his apartment.) Other than a bathroom, it really only was one big room, but designed for everything Rob needed, and its showpiece was a giant panel in the roof that rolled back at the touch of a fingertip to reveal the stars and the storms, and shut tight to seal out the sun.

"So that was how I got away from him," I said, or words to that effect. Either I was mistaken or Rob looked impatient.

"It was necessary, right? You think it was, Sherlock?" he asked.

"Why? Don't you? Are you saying I overdid it?"

"Allie, it wasn't as though Tabor was in your bedroom. It wasn't as though Bonnie wasn't there, too."

If he hadn't been so innocently beautiful, the muscles that framed his hips like narrow cords—and also indecent under the light blanket pulled up to those hips—I might have stalked out. Rob had a habit of failing me in the area of drama. "*Do you think I was over the top? Even given what he said?*"

"I think you showed off." He smiled then, his black hair falling forward over his forehead. "Come on. This bed is cold. Garrett Tabor has no place in this room." He pulled back the covers and made a place for me.

"I think I should tell someone, though, Rob," I said, obliging him by climbing in next to him and attempting to unfurl my tense body, one neuron at a time.

"Honey, if you were to tell someone, what would you tell? We've been through this."

"He taunted me with that mask . . ."

"Taunting isn't a crime. You don't even know if that was the same ski mask, Allie-Stair. In fact, I would be pretty sure it isn't. The police probably have that ski mask."

Duh. How dumb could one criminal justice major be?

Garrett Tabor had done exactly nothing except take a single step toward me. Unrecorded for posterity.

"Come here," Rob said, pulling me into the place I fit,

just in the crook of his shoulder. Before anything went further, I reminded him that I had to call my mother

"She'll be worried about me. After the other night . . . and especially since he was there." I hadn't gone into the specifics of my Corona incident, but the way news got around our town, the Dorn family had already heard about it.

Poor Jackie Kim. Her husband dumped her, a sick kid, and now this . . .

My mother had been in this *what-freak-out, that-freak-out-never-happened* mode. I knew it must have been an effort. She had switched to the three-to-eleven shift at the hospital after Juliet's death. While also working some days at the clinic on the XP Sibling Project, she was adjusting to a new circadian rhythm. Unless I was going to be home and with her, she spent most nights sleeping. She was probably asleep right now. Call? Not call?

No sooner had I finished dialing than I repented. Even leaving a message would worry Jackie. I had been the kind of daughter who didn't even call *back*, much less call to pass the time of night. Mom would cover the distance between our house and Rob's house like a falcon without benefit of wings. But . . .

"This is Jacqueline Mack Kim, co-director of the XP Sibling Project at the Tabor Clinic and After Five Emergency Services Coordinator at Divine Savior Hospital. I'm with a patient now, but will call you back promptly. If you have a life- or limb-threatening emergency, please hang up and call . . ."

Why, I will, Mom, was my first and self-centered thought. *When Tabor gets hold of a limb. And thanks.*

But my next thought was: *Thank goodness. She is asleep. She's letting it go over to voicemail.*

"I'm fine, Mom. Just wanted you to know."

Because nothing . . . really happened.

It really didn't.

My body felt as though something had happened, my brain a brushfire. It wasn't that I wanted anyone to be scared for me. Not really. Not much. I was Allie Kim, the Great and Terrible, fierce and strong. Except I wasn't even really . . . that . . . either. He scared me. He was a scary person who scared me.

I turned to Rob and smiled.

He closed his arms around me.

A WHILE LATER, staring up at the dark ceiling, I spoke. "It felt good, though."

"Thanks," Rob said lazily.

"I mean Parkour." I giggled and tried to recover. "I don't mean that being with you didn't . . . I meant . . ."

Rob sat up, rocking back once to pull on his jeans. "No offense taken. I bet it did. I bet it did. We've been hiding under a rock since that night."

Suddenly, and abruptly, I was sick of hiding.

"Why don't we do a trace?" Rob said.

"I don't want to do Parkour," I said. "If I did it for the joy, it would remind me of her, and how she died. Juliet can't feel that anymore. I couldn't experience that joy without her. Not yet. I'd be bad at it and that would be awful. Even more dangerous than it was."

"But you want to do something."

"Something risky. Some extreme gig only we can do."

Rob said slowly, "If I say I know just the thing, will you believe me?"

"Is it good? Is it scary?"

"It's good and scary, I promise," Rob said.

He had no idea.

They call it free diving, but like Parkour, it is anything but free. The price tag is steep. For starters, it's the second most dangerous sport. The first is base jumping. When people base jump, they throw themselves from cliffs, bridges, and even skyscrapers, using a parachute to break their fall. (BASE is really an acronym, meaning Buildings, Antenna, Spans, and Earth. Earth is the trick part.) Even if the parachute opens, there are times when the jumper wakes up in a full-body cast. And there are times when the jumper never wakes up at all.

There are half a dozen ways to free dive, but they all involve one thing. Or rather, they all do not involve one thing: an air supply. The breath you go down with is the breath that takes you back up.

Or so you hope.

Some people don't really dive; instead they descend on a rope to grab a flag that proves their depth conquest. Some simply go submersible in a pool for what is essentially a contest of holding their breath.

Rob and I were going to go the classic competitive way, which is called constant weight. A diver wears a belt with enough weight so that it's easier to roll your body into a pike position and go down, arms extended like Superman, kicking as little as possible as you descend (any effort uses up oxygen) until you see how low your body (and your mind, because your mind plays a big role) will allow you to go.

Free divers suffer convulsions. They pass out. They don't pause to adjust their ears and end up blowing out their eardrums.

But they love the feeling.

Why? I was going to find out why. I'd never even gone scuba diving with Rob, although he pestered me all the time to go with him.

Last summer, he was certified as an open-water diver, his way of coping with Juliet's disappearance. He'd taken instruction with Wesley, a guy legendary in Iron Harbor for his daring. Wesley had hang glided in the mountains, here and out West. He'd hiked the Appalachian Trail and then turned around and hiked back. He skydived, cave dived, and apparently, free dived, and also taught it all. He had a stack of teaching credentials—with no wall to hang them on—which was why Rob and I were on the way to see him at the Iron County YMCA pool. Rob had signed us both up for private lessons.

Rob was in a great mood.

He idolized Wesley—perhaps (not perhaps, in fact) because Wesley had unrestricted access to everything Rob had severely restricted access to—namely, the outdoors. Wesley also had that irritating nouveau hippie way of living life, so appealing to people with a Y chromosome: no girlfriend, but "special ladies" in his life, planted all over, and only in places like Maui and Taos, where he kept a bag of clothes and a bedroll stashed in their coat closets. I'd met Wesley once, in the dark—but then, almost everyone I met was in the dark—when Rob did his open-water diver's test. (Let me dis-recommend this experience to you even if you don't have XP: if you're not the one doing the test, and you're watching from the surface, watching someone take an underwater diving test makes collating paper look like a ripper of a party in Hollywood or someplace.)

Despite that not entirely thrilling experience, I was in a pretty good mood myself.

THE NIGHT BEFORE, I'd finished up my lab training with a technician, Melissa, who daylighted as an undertaker. While I couldn't assist at an autopsy, I could be an engaged observer. And luckily (though what experience that involves death can ever be considered "lucky"?) it was Bonnie's turn, although she complained that she hadn't performed an autopsy in years.

The subject was a boy, only a year older than me. There was no need to examine his two-year-old cousin, the child he had died trying to save. Drowning isn't ordinarily a suspicious death, unless there's a possibility of suicide, but both the little boy and the teenager died in shallow water. The older boy had gotten stuck under a tree root trying to reach the toddler.

"Do you think it matters, if you die alone?" I asked Bonnie.

She wasn't normally sentimental about such things, but I saw her eyes fill. She was thinking of her own son, Chris, the same age as me.

"I think it matters," she said. "I think it's better, if anything like that can be better, if you're not alone. I also think that sometimes, if you're between life and death, another person's encouragement can keep you going."

As she washed the dirt from the young man's chest, Bonnie told me that the young guy had not suffered.

"Death, itself, at the actual moment, isn't bad. In fact, it's a good feeling. People don't die, really *die*, in agony. The fear before is awful, and the knowledge. But, you've seen nature shows on TV. At the moment that the antelope in the tiger's maw lets go, the brain gives you the gift of terminal endorphins so that you can at least surrender. The agony stops. I've experienced that myself."

Between the births of her two sons, Bonnie told me she'd had a ruptured ectopic pregnancy. Apparently is one of the most painful events known to womanhood—which is, so far as I can tell, filled with them. In the ambulance, however, just before she would have died, when she'd lost so much blood that her pressure was about twelve over zero, she said she experienced a wondrous, warm euphoria, not only the cessation of the pain but the emotional assurance that her son, Chris, who was four years old, would be just fine, no matter who raised him. The paramedic, on his very first run, sensed this. When Bonnie felt his hot tears plink on her cool face, she roused herself and slipped back into achy consciousness. The medic was slapping Bonnie, and saying, *Don't die. Please don't die.* And so she didn't. Despite its manifest anguish, the experience banished any fear of actually dying that she ever had.

She quoted the poet John Peale Bishop: "Tis not death, but fear of death that restores us to the crowd."

Then, she gave me a long look and stopped the digital recorder she was wearing around her neck in a sports harness. She told me to leave.

"I'm okay," I said. "Why?"

"It's not that I don't think you're up to it. I'll make sure you do your cadaver studies on my own. It's just too soon for you, after Juliet."

I nodded. We were both thinking the same thing: *What about Juliet's dad?* Tommy Sirocco had come in with the teenage boy's family. I'd watched as Tommy turned away and pressed his hand over his eyes when the guy's mother used the corner of her sweatshirt to dry her dead son's hair. The woman's brother held her close; it had been a family vacation, and it now would be a family funeral. I left Bonnie to do her work on the cadaver and made Tommy a cup of coffee in the little break room where I did my studying. In the past three weeks, it seemed that he had lost twenty pounds. I didn't even want to ask about Juliet's mother, Ginny, who had gone to Ireland for an extended visit with her sister. When he sat down at the table, I cringed. I tried hard to grab for the book I'd left out, but he saw the cover, *The Geography of Murder.*

Embarrassed, I said, "I'm sorry."

Tommy smiled at me. His smile was worse than his expression of perpetual worry: he had always been the closest thing I'd had to a father, knuckling my head when I was little, taking me to Juliet's competitions when I was older. He peered at the book over his steaming Styrofoam cup. "I don't know this one."

"The idea is that that there are some places murderers are more likely to strike. Like Seattle."

Tommy sighed. "It makes sense. A big city near a whole lot of wilderness. Mountains. Minnesota, now, except for here, Minnesota is pretty much fields of wheat. Some forest land."

"You can hide victims in the woods."

"Yes. Sometimes. Not usually forever."

"But there are all those lakes," I said.

"You'd be surprised how difficult it is to keep a dead person missing in a lake." Tommy's face constricted when he said that, and I know we both thought of Juliet—like a wounded mermaid, draped against someone's pier, alone and waiting to be found. He took a sip and hugged my shoulder. Then he left.

"SO, WHERE DID those girls go?" I said to Rob as we turned up Harbor Road to the YMCA. "It's not just that Tabor blends in and feels safe. It's that he picks his victims wisely. They all do. Those girls in the apartments could have been runaways. They could have been tourists. They could have been hookers from Thunder Bay. Where are they now, though? He didn't leave them in that apartment. He didn't kill them there."

Rob hadn't said much the whole ride. He wasn't curious; he was impatient. I knew that he wanted our time together to be a break from all things Tabor. But I couldn't help telling the most important person in my life what was on my mind, could I?

"It's a where-done-it," Rob said, with a twitch of his lips that tried for a smile. "Who would know better than Tabor, because of his father being Dr. Stephen, how to remove anything that would tie him to a crime or to . . . anyone."

"He knows how to get rid of evidence. And he knows this place, every inch. He controls it. How many times has he gotten away with it, Rob?"

"Honey, I know this question eats away at you. I know it does. But we've said all this before, Allie, and I can't count how many times." Rob let out a gusty breath and parked the

Tanganyika in East Africa and Lake Baikal in Siberia are bigger. I would bet, however, that people in Siberia are not walking around in sixty-below-zero weather trading zingers about Baikal's sheer size, the way people do here—where it only gets to be about thirty below.

"You know, you could put the state of Maine in Lake Superior," I said to Rob as he locked up his car.

"Good thing we're only going swimming in a pool tonight."

"And in the deepest spot? If you put the Sears Tower right down in that hole, only a few of the floors would be sticking out."

"Imagine that."

"But here's what's really interesting. If you drained it, you could cover all of North America and South America, too, with one or two feet of water."

"Both of them?"

"Yep. Alberta to Argentina."

And yes, that is so way not normal by any definition, to be so mystified by a hole with water in it that isn't Loch Ness.

Rob just grinned. But I knew he was with me. There is something mystifying about the lake.

You can't ignore it. You belong to it. Every day that I got closer to thinking of myself within Lake Superior's own life story, I thought of all the lives that Lake Superior had taken into itself—in peril or simply in the way of things, with time. Hundreds and thousands. A great bowl of ghosts.

Superior never gives up her dead.

Down into that lake I was intending to go, for Rob. The love of my guy, Rob. He was lucky he had a sense of humor and unmanageable black curls because I would absolutely not be doing this for anyone else.

We arrived at the Y, and I caught myself repeating for the hundredth time: *Tonight, it's only a pool, Allie. It's the pool.*

"Ready to test your limits?" said a pebbly voice behind us.

I jumped about three feet straight up, and whirled around. There was the Famous Wesley. I let out a deep breath.

Wesley was one of those older guys who seemed cut from some kind of root, bleached brows over startling blue eyes, his nose and cheeks spare and brown as planes of teak. The only thing fat about him was his shoulder-length hair, plaited in a loose braid that managed to look utilitarian instead of affected. He could have been a Harvard MBA but would always look like he'd spent the night in a backpacker tent on a surfer beach in Malibu (which I've never seen but imagine) or Maui (which I've also never seen but imagine even more often). Surfing and diving, and camping and hiking, and taking photographs that looked like museum art with a camera from RadioShack—this was what Wesley did. According to Rob, Wesley also ate voraciously, four burgers at a sitting, five bowls of chili.

Still, he was literally concave.

According to Rob, Wesley's secret was that he didn't eat on a regular basis, and what he did eat, he ate at Gitchee Gumee Pizza or at Sprouting Life, the natural food store. He lived in a cabin on the backside of Torch Mountain that was half ruin and half rehab. It had no electricity or plumbing. He had paid nine hundred dollars for it. He did, however, have great teeth (gift of a concerned mother, I would bet) and a great smile, which he turned on me as he held out one big hand.

"Last time I was diving, was with Gary," Wesley said. "You know Gary Tabor?"

"Kind of," I said, feeling electricity sizzle along my legs

and pounce across the space between us to Rob. I could barely stand still.

Wouldn't it be?

Wouldn't it just be?

"A great man," Wesley said, and I could almost hear Rob's silent groan at the unsolicited endorsement of my future murderer. Still, Wesley seemed good-humored and genuine, and was not by far the first to be hoodwinked by Tabor. "It's a coincidence that we went diving that day last summer, because you guys have the sunlight thing, right?"

"Yep, we're from the dark side," Rob said.

"Because Gary was telling me, there's all new work he's doing on XP. He's at the head of that."

"Hardly at the head of it," I muttered. "He's just a nurse who does a little lab work. His father and his uncle are the real researchers." I sounded like a brat and couldn't help myself.

"But he puts in the time," Wesley said. "He really cares."

"So you went diving? Free diving?" Rob said, in a fast attempt to diffuse the tension and slice through the rind of animosity coming from me. Wesley didn't seem to feel it at all.

"Scuba," said Wesley. "We went into some of those caves under the old boathouse where the condominiums are. Where Gary lives." Serene with the power of the virtuous, I only smiled. Ah, the sweet irony: having promised not to speak Garrett Tabor's name, only to have somebody do it for me. "And then we looked over the Gracie J., that old boat they sank when the part of the cliff went in? The boat and the old boathouse, that's awesome structure for fish. About sixty feet down. You could make that a goal. It's quiet there, with those two arms of rock making a cove." He spread his own arms side. "We saw a sturgeon, must have been seventy pounds, man."

I grimaced. "I sure did not sign up to see that," I said. Sturgeons are huge, ancient creatures, pebbled all over like alligators. The thought of them cruising around under me, or worse, past me, made me want to jump back in Rob's van and go back to his apartment and hide with him under the covers.

"They aren't sharks!" Rob said, trying not to laugh.

"Do they know that?" I squeaked. He did laugh then. We all did.

"Let's go for a dive, huh, kids?" Wesley said. "No sturgeons at the Y, I promise."

A HALF-HOUR LATER, Rob and I were suited up and in the water, which was freezing. I couldn't stop shivering, even though both of us wore body suits and scuba masks. Wesley wore cutoffs. He was chatty. Maybe he wasn't used to being here all alone in the middle of the night, because he seemed to get a kick out of it.

He also told us that he'd gone to high school with "Gary" Tabor.

"I thought you were a lot younger," Rob said.

"No, I probably just look it. It's because I don't have a mortgage or kids. If you sit light on the land, it's usually pretty easy on you, too. I'm not like a professional man. When it comes times for me to fade back into the land, well, I won't have much to leave or far to go."

I hate it when people say shit like that. Still, Wesley had a kind of irresistible sweetness about him that overrode the eye roll that is usually my reflex response.

"Are you friends now?" I asked, trying to remember if I was supposed to pinch my nose or push down to clear my mask. I was sure that I was supposed to pantomime blowing my nose to depressurize my ears, and do this every few feet, even in the pool.

"We go way back. He's a busy man," Wesley said. "Very busy man."

"I'll say," I agreed.

"He coached the Everson twins," Wesley went on, referring to brothers from Iron Harbor who now skied on the Canadian national team. "And that poor kid, Juliet Sirocco."

I resisted the urge to cry out. Murderous now on my own, I turned to stare at Rob, who kept his eyes on Wesley. I knew what he would say if I challenged him later, asking how Wesley, *who had taught Rob his open-water diving skills at the same time Juliet died*, didn't know about us in relation to Juliet? He would say what he always said. *Guys don't talk about stuff like that.*

Wesley walked away to get weight belts.

"You are an asshole for not telling me he knew our friend 'Gary,'" I whispered furiously to Rob.

"Because I didn't know he knew him? Guys don't take out their phones and compare all their contacts to see if they match."

"So what do guys talk about?"

"What's in front of them," Rob said. He grinned. "Like a hot girl. Or, like, kinds of beer."

I scowled and turned away. Frustrated, I made the choice to wad up all the thoughts of resentment like damp paper and stow them.

"Now, the first recorded free diver did his thing maybe sixty or seventy years ago," Wesley said, rejoining us at poolside. "In the Aegean, I think, there was this guy who dived for an anchor and everybody thought he was dead, when he came popping back up. With the anchor! He was submerged for something like six minutes. Nobody had ever really measured that, although sponge divers and pearl divers were familiar with it, of course. This guy had two busted ear drums and a heart about three times the size it should have been for a little-sized guy."

"And?" I asked, puzzled. I wasn't following.

"Well, large hearts pump slower, and the slower your heart goes, the less oxygen you use. Right?"

"Oh," I said. "So it shouldn't be that bad, if you're fit. And we're pretty fit."

"If it was just your heart and your lungs and your legs, and your flexibility and your strength, it wouldn't be bad at all," Wesley said.

"What else is there?" Rob guessed. "Your ears?"

"What's between your ears. It's all about your head. Because the fear factor is real. You have a whole lot more oxygen in you than you realize, but if you start to freak out, your body is going to demand to breathe. You have to over-come the buildup of carbon dioxide that makes you want to . . . well, gasp for breath. Any person in good shape can endure apnea for two minutes or more. But after that, when your body tries to take over, it's a head game."

Rob nodded. "That's why people hyperventilate before they free dive. I saw it in a French film."

"You watched a *French film*?" I said. "You watched a *French film* about diving? Because knowing you, the only kind of French film you'd watch . . ."

"I'm a cultured person," Rob replied, batting his long lashes at me. "These divers were world champions. And they basically huffed and puffed multiple times . . ."

"That was a movie. Divers do that if they're extremely stupid instead of just extreme, if they want to die," Wesley said. "You can throw off carbon dioxide that way but you risk an SWB."

"What's that?" I said.

"A shallow water blackout," said Wesley.

I asked the obvious, as I was slipping into the blade-like fins as long as my arm. "Why did it happen in shallow water, like . . . why would you fall in the last part of the race?"

"The body is tired. You're depleted mentally. And there are other science reasons."

Wesley's use of terms like "other science reasons" didn't exactly inspire soaring confidence. The side of the ledger with black marks ticking off *Ways I Definitely Do Not Want to Die* began filling up.

"You can have a deep water blackout, too. Either way, you just drown."

Hmmm.

Either way, you drown. For every point in the ledger of going water wacky with my beloved, there were now ten points in the other column.

Wesley smiled. "That's why you're supersafe when you free dive for more than a couple of minutes. That's why you have someone with scuba gear to check you out as you go down, and stay with you. No one's going to let you drown, Allie."

Hmm. This removed maybe . . . one black mark.

Lake Superior's Titanic-sinking coldness was actually to our advantage. If you put your face in a bowl of cold water, or even splash cold water on your face, your heart rate and circulation slows, because of this evolutionary inheritance called the mammalian diving reflex. It's the reason that small kids can sometimes be revived after long minutes at the bottom of a pool. In cold water, the need to breathe, at least the physical need, is actually decreased. I thought for a moment of the little boy in the shallow lake. That had been cold water; nobody was even supposed to be swimming. The fathers were fishing, hoping to catch dinner in water that was crisping at the edges with ice. It would have seemed such a simple matter for the older guy to jump in and pull the little kid out . . . how could the older boy have died so quickly in such cold water? With the family all there thrashing around? The mammalian body knows how to conserve the oxygen for the tissues that need it most—mostly the brain. Hence the autopsy, I guess . . . I dragged myself back to the water at hand.

Wesley was saying that if we were going scuba diving, we'd need dry suits to withstand the epic cold down there because we'd be cruising around, looking at the ribs of dead boats. But for a free dive, we'd only need ordinary wet suits, masks, and these huge blade-like fins to get us the farthest down with the least amount of kicking—which depletes oxygen.

For now, we just practiced sitting on the bottom of the pool with a weight belt on that wasn't heavy enough to keep us from kicking to the surface. Which I did. I kicked to the surface after fifty seconds and air never felt so good.

"Rob must have unusually large lungs for his body size," Wesley said, as Rob edged past a minute. "What he's doing is what you have to do, Allie. You have to clear your mind to the edges."

As if.

Another twenty or forty points in the *Do-Not-Want-to-Die* column.

As I stood there shivering and staring at Rob, sitting contentedly *underwater,* Wesley told me about a Russian diver, Natalia Molchanova, who could hold her breath for eight minutes. In 2009, she finally became the first woman to break the record of free diving a hundred meters (that's more than three hundred feet, folks). She actually dived *one hundred and one* meters, just for insurance. According to Wesley, an American woman, Sara Campbell, had done it first. But Campbell didn't get to keep her record. The rules say (and who made up these rules?) that you have to remain conscious for sixty seconds on the surface after you make your dive. Sara Campbell got back to the surface, took two breaths, and passed out.

Fifty more points in the *No-Way-in-Hell* column for that kind of anecdote.

"As breath holders go, Sara Campbell isn't really great," Wesley said. "Five minutes maybe."

"What about you?" I asked, teasing, trying to avoid thinking about Rob, who had now gone over two minutes without breathing.

"Me? Three minutes maybe? I'm about the dive and what you see, not the immersion."

Wesley reached into his pocket for his phone and showed me a picture of Sara Campbell at the bottom of the sea, wearing a dive suit that had a single huge fin. She looked exactly like a mermaid, but with a sleek hood and mask instead of the fabled flowing locks. She was looking straight at the camera, calmly. It was like one of those pictures where you try to find the hidden drawing of a shell or a ruler except instead of there being something there that shouldn't be, there was something missing. People photographed at the bottom of the sea usually have on a breathing apparatus or are in agony or are obviously dead.

"If you read about Sara Campbell, she passes out pretty often," he said, shoving his phone back in his pocket "She doesn't really mind it. She says she kind of likes the feeling."

He paused. "She says that she thinks of being in an Alpine meadow. Puts a whole new perspective on death, doesn't it?"

And ten more black marks in the Ixnay ledger.

"That woman who can do it for eight minutes? What does she think about?" I asked.

"Nothing," said Wesley.

"Like meditation?"

"No, really nothing at all. You have to be so still that some people free dive with their eyes closed."

"Now, that sounds like a ton of fun."

"Not for me, but they dig the concentration experience. Thinking about nothing is not easy," he said. "Like, during meditation, you're free. You can breathe or move. It's only frustrating if you break out of your trance state." Why had I ever doubted that Wesley was a meditator as well? He could probably meditate while holding *Vrksasana*. "When you free dive, if you break the focus, you don't just get annoyed. You could get hurt."

That we were able to have this whole conversation while my boyfriend was underwater, not breathing, seemed only to prove to me that Wesley was in his own trance state. Just when I felt I would scream, Rob finally surfaced, not even really lunging. He slapped the water as though he'd medaled in the 200-meter free.

I stretched out to kiss him. "I was a little scared, honey. How did you do it? What's in it for you?"

"Power," Rob said. "I have power over this body that's always had way too much power over me."

I never loved him more than right then.

SO, ALTHOUGH I wasn't psyched the way I was with Parkour, I decided to start trying to build up my own—this sounds weird—daily apnea practice. I was ready to try something new, something that really did have nothing to do with Juliet or Garrett Tabor, or the death I encountered nightly at my volunteer job. There is something undeniable about the dream of youth, of being young. I saw it in Wesley's eyes, the way he looked at us with wistful longing. You can store old pain that pulses new every day, like a solar cell—and, at the same time, spellbound by your own body and blood, you arch eagerly toward the future.

We agreed to come on Thursday and Saturday nights, when I didn't work. Rob and I would start by sitting on the bottom, looking into each other's eyes. Then we'd cruise back and forth on the bottom in the deep end, trying to expend as little energy as possible.

At first, I had to fight off hysteria.

Gradually, though, I learned to think of nothing, as Wesley had advised. Thinking of nothing refreshes you, although it is hideously hard doing it. Maybe it *was* a sort of trance state. The closest thing I can compare it to is hypnosis, which I've never experienced. Still, bit by bit, I grew to crave that power over my body that so beguiled Rob. We grew closer, with that sense of tribe we'd loved with Parkour—the supreme, almost smug, thrill of being *us*: close together and in the throes of something fierce. And I began to crave the real thing, beyond the pool.

Our nights assumed a kind of purposeful rhythm, based on the desire to dive in Lake Superior before school started again for me.

Wesley warned us: be patient. We wanted to be not ready, but more than ready, when we actually tried a deep dive. "The future comes soon enough," he said.

If only it never had.

6

NIGHT LIGHTS

NIGHT LIGHTS

My twenty days of volunteer service ended.

I had, however, done a good job: the ultimate frozen lemonade made from the ultimate lemons of life.

With Dr. Stephen's permission by proxy (he was still away in Bolivia), Bonnie hired me as a junior assistant, several nights each week until school resumed at the end of January, and then Friday and Saturday nights during the school year. It was good money, and while most girls wouldn't want to spend four hours of their weekend nights in a morgue, I wasn't most girls.

"I told you good would come from this," my mother said.

"I would have rather had it come on a different train," I told her.

Still, it wasn't all bad. Bonnie was smart and kind, as was mortuary Melissa, whom Rob referred to as Morticia. I loved the awe-inspiring poignancy and responsibility that came with answering questions the dead would ask, if they could. Bonnie taught me practical things, such as all the things that petechia could mean, from mononucleosis to alcoholism to lupus to death by strangulation, and how those things sometimes got mixed up. She taught me that hydrogen cyanide can be very hard to detect after death, unless the investigators find residue. A man who had moved to Iron Harbor with his wife from China had slowly poisoned himself accidentally by ingesting arsenic. Over the course of years he had eaten great quantities of rice grown near arsenic-contaminated wells. His wife was fine. She simply didn't like rice.

Each morning, after I got off work and before we went to sleep, together or separately (both our parents politely looked the other way), Rob and I trained. We did yoga, for balance, strength, and concentration. We did "apnea walks," to teach ourselves to cope sanely with the feeling of oxygen deprivation. We'd do a big "breathe-up," (or filling a lunger), followed by a short breath and hold, all at rest. Still holding our breath, we would then walk as far as we could until we absolutely had to breathe. Since both of us were athletes, we could go almost a hundred yards that way, our muscles getting more and more accustomed to working without oxygen.

We also ran and sang, simultaneously. We'd learned that this was a good way to build your lung capacity.

Down the back roads of Iron Harbor, up onto the ridges, past the unoccupied summer houses, we ran, sometimes on crusts of snow that melted away in the still freakishly warm winter weather. We sang our way through classic Motown, newer Motown, old ABBA, even older CCR, anything with a beat that required holding a note, from Boston to Beyoncé to Bruno Mars. Finally, we worked our way up—or down, if you want to look at it that way— to show tunes. That didn't last long. Garret Tabor didn't hang around anymore very much, but he would show up some nights unexpectedly at the medical examiner's office. One night, I heard him whistling "The Sound of Music," and I knew it was meant to telegraph to me that he knew what Rob and I were doing. That very thought was appalling. Did he watch me all the time?

NOT LONG AFTER that night, about four in the morning, we were running on Shore Road. We were past Tabor Oaks, down on one of the little beaches along that same stretch of highway, when Rob quietly put his hands on my arm.

"Stop running and be quiet," he said. "Just fade back behind that little bit of birch and look over there."

Far to our left, we could see what appeared to be a diver.

There could not be another human being as melon-ball nuts as Rob and me. What was somebody doing out in the lake alone in the middle of the night? It wasn't a rescue diver, because there were no lights or vans or any other equipment set up. And who ever dived alone? Crouched quietly, we watched the distant person make what Rob called a shore entry (the other kind of scuba entry, which was tipping backward or taking a big scissor walk out of a boat) and slip away into the dark water. The only sign of the person was a series of lighted flats that were presumably tethered to buoys. We watched for a long time, but our heated-up muscles were starting to knot up painfully, and even in winter, night doesn't last forever. So we turned and jogged back to Rob's Jeep and headed toward home and a hot soak before sleep.

THE NEXT NIGHT, at the pool, I was mermaiding along the deep-end bottom when suddenly, it hit me like a piano dropped from the penthouse.

Rob thought I was in trouble when I started pointing to

the surface like a crazy person, dragging on his arms, finally pinching him.

When we broke the surface, I gasped, "I know where he keeps them! That was him! That's where they are!"

Although he knew what I meant, Rob had a cooler head than my own. "Okay, sure. Allie, I'll think that over."

"Think it over? We have to go down there!"

Wesley appeared at the side of the pool. "What? You guys find buried treasure?"

Rob said, "Oh, no, man. It's nothing. Just . . . some things we lost in the dark one night."

7

THINGS YOU'D
RATHER NOT KNOW

That night, as we drove home from the Y, we were both
tired and famished. Swimming hunger makes you
deranged: I could have killed a deer and roasted it on the hood
of the car. I wanted to curl up at 9 P.M. with my blankie in the
middle the night like some Daytimer. Still, my realization at
the bottom of the pool had opened a pure adrenaline IV. Had
I tried to lie down for a nap, all my conjectures would have
kept on gyrating around the ring in my brain like electrons in
a synchrotron until I glowed.

Most stereotypes are obnoxious, but a few have earned
the gold standard of truth. One is that girls do talk more
than guys do. Our brains seem to issue press releases every
few minutes whether we like it or not. It's our way of trying
to figure out the trajectory of the universe so that we can
alter it. Girls firmly believe this is in our power, whether it
requires intellect, pure force, stealth, or berry lip stain. Rob
once told me that guys don't talk as much because guys are
here now, in the present— like Zen-ing. They're watching the

passing parade. He said that men think of the universe and time like an escalator. They're on it, and it's either going up or it's going down, but they can no more control its course than they can see who's running the machine. Any girl would consider that foolishness.

So, as soon as Rob and I got into the car, he wanted to talk food and I wanted to talk homicide. Crackling with frustration, I waited until we were in Rob's mother's kitchen.

Soon, we had assembled double-stuff pimento cheese and pickle sandwiches and potato soup so thick it was like a colloid, and I then became absorbed with my stomach's primal demands. When those were satiated, and we'd gone up to Rob's place, Rob got interested in other primal demands and was persistent and skillful enough so that those demands became urgent for me, as well.

AFTERWARD, LYING UNDER the sweep of stars in bed, it would have been so easy to dismiss all that nasty jazz about cold and watery tombs. But Rob didn't love me just for my body. Although my preoccupation with other people's, the blue-white and decomposing kind, wasn't a particular attraction.

"Hey you," I said. "What Wesley said about the structure, all those sunken boats?"

"What?" he mumbled.

"Rob! That's where he hides things. People. Dead bodies. That's Tabor's stash. He was that diver. You know it."

"That doesn't make sense, Allie. If Tabor didn't want to get caught, he'd scatter the bodies all over the hills. I hate to say this, but a part here and a part there—"

"No, no!" I broke in, sitting up under the covers. "Don't think in terms of regular person sense. A regular person would think in a different way. That's what they do. Serial killers like having a habitat. They visit their kills. They dig them up and sometimes they even . . ."

Rob actually paled. "If what's coming is what I think is coming, do not go there. I don't have your capacity for mayhem. I'm going to major in computer programming."

I almost smiled. "Okay, but see my point? He was going to visit those corpses. So many of them do that. They're driven to."

"Allie, what I love about you is you're just so damn cuddly, aren't you? All roses and pink ribbons."

"Pardon me. I didn't know those were your expectations."

"Let's just let it go for a little while, Allie Bear. I just want a little nap."

Juliet had called me Allie Bear. Rob might have thought he was pouring on the soothing syrup, but on this girl's fire, it was lighter fluid.

I was desperate.

I got up and put on Rob's shirt.

Here is another stereotype that may not bolster the image of young guys as fragile emotional beings able to conquer their desires in most circumstances, and yet it's a stereotype that glows with authenticity. One hour after running the Death Valley marathon, a guy will stand to attention for a girl wearing his shirt over nothing else.

And Rob did. He sat up and slapped on an expression that said: I'm committed. It didn't matter if he really was serious, it only mattered that he acted like he was. I would settle for Rob being along for the ride, because Rob along for the ride was as good as most people's complete commitment. An Oscar-winning fake could trump the real thing:

Otherwise, why would half the people in Iron Harbor trust Garrett Tabor?

"That's where those girls' bodies are, Rob. It's like this was meant to be. Tabor hides them down there. Remember I started babysitting at the condos? Remember? And I saw him standing out on the lawn and he had something, like a sail, folded up on the ground. But what if it wasn't a sail? What if it was a girl's body, wrapped in a sheet?"

"What if it was an old sail wrapped in a sheet?"

When I'd called the police that time, they'd found the old door, a kind of hatch entrance to the long-gone boathouse.

"But he disappeared, Rob! He went down that door that Dr. Stephen had nailed up later. What if he went back and pulled it apart? It wouldn't be so hard. What if he uses that old door in the ground like his own trapdoor to hell? That book I was reading? About murder and geography? People would dump dead bodies in lakes all over Minnesota if it weren't so hard to keep bodies hidden in lakes. But Superior's different from other lakes."

"Wait," Rob said. "Slow down. What book?"

"I told you about that book ages ago. Jesus! Whole civilizations have risen and fallen since I told you about it!" I'm not a patient person. You may have intuited that.

"I don't remember."

But I was thinking harder now, thoughts literally humming like notes on a big chord organ. What if Tabor actually brought victims—their bodies—to the actual medical examiner's office? What kind of a pimp would that be? What if somebody walked in? He could just cover the body with a sheet or put it in the filing cabinet of death, those refrigerated drawers. I said, "Rob! He knows there's no video cameras in that office. The only cameras are the Polaroids they use during an autopsy. The only recording devices are the microphones they use to describe autopsy findings, when they weigh and measure, you know, people's parts."

"Allie! You're spinning like the hubcaps on my dad's old Camaro! Just slow down!"

If only I had a dollar for every time someone has told me to slow down. Or even a penny. I'd be a freaking thousandaire.

"Were you even listening?"

"I was."

"Well, your buddy Wesley said Gary's an expert diver. And you know that serial killers . . ."

"You mentioned that. They want to revisit their . . . kills. The whole thought is beyond me, but okay."

"This would be a really unique way for him to visit his kills," I said. "So we have to go down there. It can't be too deep. Maybe thirty feet. The perfect dive."

"The dive is the point of the dive," Rob said.

"People free dive all the time to spear fish and stuff."

"We were going to do it for the dive itself."

"Oh, come on, we'll do a dive that's pure first, and . . . and then can we look?"

"You'll feel like it's wasted time, won't you?" Rob said.

"Not really."

We both knew that I was lying.

8

CHILLING
CHILLING

Without Garrett Tabor's constant presence, life at the medical examiner's office with Bonnie and Melissa, the technician, was pleasant—if you can say such a thing. Did I develop a callous on my sensibilities with regard to death, its sights and messages?

I did.

My experiences began to harden me—not my core personality, but a slice of my outer being, to a degree that shocked Rob and bugged my mother.

To be honest, I also was actively trying to bug my mother.

Maybe you can explain the psychology of this; I can't. I wanted her to be mad at me because I was so afraid of this new sport Rob and I had undertaken.

Little things about it kept shearing my nerves.

For one thing, our first free dive should have been uneventful.

Wesley had dropped a rope with an anchor to the bottom of a small, clear, familiar lake, The Little Cauldron. Holding the rope, he went down first, wearing scuba gear and a head-lamp (we had on waterproof, mini miners lights over our hoods, as well). Next, all three of us made the slow descent, but only Wesley was breathing.

We went down thirty feet, not quite ten meters, into The Little Cauldron, where we sat on the bottom and mimed clinking champagne glasses.

Then, at two minutes and fourteen seconds—despite all the yoga, despite the über-concentration on the Zen of thinking of absolutely nothing, despite all those apnea walks, despite understanding that my aerobic capacity far out-stripped my reflexive urge to gasp, despite knowing that once I hit three minutes (as I had four times in training) I would experience a solid, eerie calm—I panicked.

What you really experience isn't the urge to inhale, it's the urge to *exhale*. The carbon dioxide is intolerable. I couldn't pull myself together enough to fight it. Bubbles burst from my lips; I wrenched away and kicked for the surface like a crazy person, and Wesley had to hold me down and let me buddy-breathe from his regulator so that I could settle down long enough to equalize the pressure in my ears. Rob looked up at me and made sure I signaled I was okay, then he completed, serenely rising.

Wesley comforted me at the surface. He said this was normal. Then again, he would have said it was normal if I'd surfaced with my tongue wrapped around my ear lobe, too. "This is no reason to delay a deep dive," he said. "I'll be with you, and you will do just fine."

Except when that night came, I didn't think we would do just fine. I thought I would die, and so I picked a fight with my mother.

Later, I realized that I thought subconsciously that if she was mad at me when I died, she wouldn't miss me so much.

THE MOMENT I woke up, I knew something would go wrong.

My mom's brother, my uncle Brian, who's a basketball coach, once told me that he could tell when he got out of bed if he was going to sprain his ankle. I got out of bed that night with a sprained-ankle feeling. I knew something bad would go down, but I thought it would be that I'd lose it again, or have ear problems. In the days before, I'd slept restlessly. I had the sick shivers of bad sleep, and, because you can never eat when you're jittery, I was hungry and also semi-outraged at the thought of food, at the idea of even chewing and swallowing.

I was stuck on all those stupid statistics, on the presence of a lake the size of a small nation. How prepared I was physically not only to survive but thrive in my dive was all pudding . . . until I thought about the Sears Tower with only a couple of floors sticking out. Even though I wasn't going down more than fifty feet. Maybe not that deep. Why did people have to say stuff like that? Like, if you jumped to your death from the Golden Gate Bridge, it would take you seven seconds to hit? Seven seconds is a damn long time to think.

There's stuff you just don't want to know.

After that night, I knew for a certainty that there's stuff you don't want to know no matter how much you think you do.

Moreover, I hated that I had nudged Rob to use our brief time underwater as a detective mission—to get a little glimpse at some of that structure and those caves Wesley had described. I figured that Rob could do some kind of computer simulation of the exact spot where we saw the lone diver, relative to the place Wesley had described the wreckage of the boat and the old boathouse. That way, we could move quickly.

I brought this up a few nights before at a very propitious moment. "Remember, I said I thought that I knew where Tabor kept . . ."

"Fine," Rob said, standing up and reverse stripping. Playtime was over. Rob's dad brought home team swag without respect for creed or religion, and Rob wore them that way, too. Tonight he was wearing a Patriots hoodie with Green Bay Packers pants.

"Wherever those girls are, those girls are Juliet," I said. "I couldn't find her but maybe . . ."

"I'll try to make a map," Rob said. "I said I would."

THEN CAME THE appointed time. When I sat down for dinner, I started nattering about a suicide—the second suicide in less than a month.

"It shows you what kind of mood people are in, in our picturesque little hamlet the week before Christmas," I said. "Bet there are more suicides in Minnesota than in any other state."

"That would be Wyoming," my mother said placidly. "That is the state with the most suicides."

"But what about the Norwegian temperament . . . ?"

"The top ten countries with the most suicides are not in Scandinavia. That's a myth. The places with the most suicides per capita are all part of Russia or Eastern Europe," said Jackie. "As for states, Minnesota is number . . . forty. No, I'm wrong. It's forty-one."

"How do you know that?"

"I pay attention," she said.

"What about the sub-zero cold, and the darkness, and the boredom, and the mosquitoes?"

"They must build character," Jackie said.

"What about the fatness?" Angie put in. "Mrs. Haven says there are more fat people in Minnesota than in any other state."

"She's wrong," said my mother, the walking wiki. "That's Mississippi."

I was tired of all this determined cheer. "So I was saying: last night we hosted an old married couple."

My mother knew I meant at the morgue. Jackie gave me the kind of warning look meant to be doubly threatening coupled with a paring knife. She was only slicing green peppers. But still. I was already committed to bugging her, so I went on. The couple, in their eighties, took an overdose of sleeping pills, mailing a letter to the sheriff's office at the time they did it. The wife was dying of cancer. The husband died of the habit of loving her.

My mother found this romantic.

I found it absurd.

"They had children," I said. "It was rude to put themselves first."

"If they were in their eighties, the children were grown and independent," my mother said.

"It's still thoughtless," I said. "I'd be pissed at you."

"I'm not the type," Jackie said. "But if you've spent an entire lifetime with someone . . ."

The last time I'd visited my mom at the ER, she'd been flirting. She was flirting with a guy young enough that she could have been his babysitter when she was in seventh grade. Jackie was the kind of fit, sassy, almost-forty woman that men both a whole lot younger and a whole lot older found very attractive. She'd introduced me to the doctor she was flirting with as "my daughter, who's a freshman in college," and he made all the obligatory get-the-crash-cart-how-can-you-have-a-kid-that-old gestures, and his name was . . . Colby. Not his last name, either. This went down like fishhooks with me. My mother had a right to date, but she had a right to date guys named "Jim" or "Paul." Not "Colby." Colby belonged to the kind of generation—and, well, the kind of parent—who would have tats and name their kids Lee and Ryder, after kinds of jeans. Or Bevin and Bryce and Bella Roma or something, so they all matched.

"Would you give your life for Rob?" Jackie asked me.

"No," I said. "I wouldn't even think of it. Rob has XP. He's time-limited, basically, even though he's the most important person in my life."

Jackie said dryly, "Really."

I didn't know if she was saying "really" about the time-limited part or the not-giving-my-life part or about his being my life's only. I chose the latter. Your family doesn't like to hear that your boyfriend is your breath. They want to still pretend they come first with you, like when you were six. That I sometimes did feel that way made me all the crankier.

"Aside, obviously, from you guys," I said. "I would give my life for you, Mom, or Angela, but I wouldn't expect you to do the same . . ."

"Oh," Jackie said. "That's droll."

I didn't even know what "droll" meant.

"But I have XP, too. It would be a waste of your . . . whatever. Your protective heroism."

Jackie slammed the salad bowl down on the table so hard that the salad dressings sloped to the sides of their containers like the water around those little ships in bottles. She clearly had been saving up for a fight since I'd flipped out in the street and stolen the poncho. If I went along with it, which I'd decided I would, it would be a doozy. How patient and gentle my mother could be with some smelly woodsy drunk who'd split his head open trying to light a cigar while standing on a fire hydrant. But with me . . . She said, "Pardon me for my naïve belief that even people with chronic illnesses are worth saving, even risking your life for. If you love them. I'm in a medical field, you see."

I shrugged. "I guess it goes with the territory."

"And as for those old people? They took vows. I'm not saying a healthy person should take his own life because his partner is dying, but they took those vows seriously. Most people don't."

By most people, she meant my father.

Sometimes it's just satisfying to piss your mother off, so she doesn't get the idea that because you have a handicap and need to be around her most of the time, you're best friends or something. My mother and I already got along uncomfortably well—although all I would need to do was to tip my hand about free diving and all those special moments would swiftly be Xed out and, almost-college freshman or not, I would find myself confined to base camp.

Parkour was one thing. The previous night, Rob and I had watched a documentary about free diving in which divers sawed through foot-thick ice in Greenland to erect a little teepee thing that they used as their dive platform. Since she'd personally held together the edges of bellies torn out by the actions of people who actually had gone ballistic, Jackie didn't appreciate that term much either, so I used it.

I said, "Don't go ballistic. That kind of love just seems obsessive."

"You're not a mother," said my mother in a voice that was too quiet.

"And those old people, they . . . you know, they left the heat on. Which, why would you do if you were going to off yourself? They semi-decomposed and wrecked the whole cabin. Now their kids will never even be able to go there and remember the happy times. They'll have to burn the place."

"You're all heart, Allie," Mom said. "And I don't know that I appreciate this level of dinner conversation with Angela here. In fact, I'm not that hungry anymore either."

She got up and went upstairs to her office, slamming the door.

I got up and grabbed my backpack, filled with diving gear. I called Rob to pick me up and slammed the door experimentally a couple of times to see if my mother noticed. I'd won, but I felt as though I'd lost. Angela got up gratefully because she hated tofu and pea pods.

I went outside to wait. We were to meet Wesley at ten o'clock, when he finished Pilates or Sufi dancing or whatever he was teaching that week, so we had time to kill. Rob finally showed up, shortly before my lashes froze and broke off in little black commas of ice.

We drove through town, all festive for Christmas, just four days away, looking as though someone had salted the whole place with a gigantic shaker filled with white twinkle lights.

We went to Gitchee Gumee Pizza to eat a meat lover's with extra onion—and the thought of how much it would piss off my mother was as much of a delight as the chopped steak, hot sausage, and pepperoni. For Jackie Kim, exercise and nutrition were sacred, like the Stations of the Cross were for my devoutly Catholic Grandma Mack. She wanted to instill her religious vegetarian fervor in her hedonistic daughter. No chance at that, though. I was born carnivorous and got meat on the street whenever I could.

As we ate, Gideon Brave Bear, Gitchee's owner, brought us underage draft beers and sat with us for a round. Except for Juliet's funeral, we hadn't seen him, since he'd fired a gun into the air in Garrett Tabor's direction last summer after Tabor chased me from the cemetery right into the middle of town. Then, I thought he was trying to kill me. I still thought he was trying to kill me, but he was taking his time.

"Are you doing good enough, Allie?" Gid asked me, exactly the right question in exactly the right way.

"Good enough, Gid. Thanks," I said, laying my shockingly white hand over his own.

After Gid went back to the bar, I told Rob about the suicides and my mother's typically overboard reaction. "I just said, no offense, but to me that kind of love is borderline."

Rob rolled the foam on his beer around the top of the tall glass. "No offense, Allie, but that was a pretty shitty thing to say."

At first, I thought I hadn't heard him right. Then, I couldn't believe that Rob would just cut me loose like that when it came to parents and their default smothering. "Shitty? Of me? It is obsessive! Your parents do the same thing!"

"But why wouldn't they? Of course, they're obsessed with their kid, especially the way things are with us. Do you blame your mom for wanting to keep you healthy and to be with you every minute she can? You're acting like she holds you down and she won't let you out of the house."

"She wouldn't let me out if she could get away with it."

Even I knew that was a lie.

"That's unfair, honey. We kind of owe it to them to cut them a little slack, Allie. Or the reverse of cutting them a little slack. They give their whole lives for us and it has to suck for them."

I sighed, and said, "Okay."

"You can be confrontational, Allie."

"I am not," I said, getting up and getting ready to walk out on him. Which was pretty confrontational. "I guess . . . I guess I am. Lately anyhow. I didn't used to be this way. I woke up tonight all freaked out, Rob. I don't know why. I'm freaked out about free diving. I never felt like that about Parkour.

"You'll be fine. You're letting it stress you out. It's a head trip," Rob said.

"I'm also afraid of what we might find if we look around."

"Then, honey, let's not look around. Let's do something just for us."

"But we planned . . ."

"I'm not saying never. Just how about not tonight? Let's have conversations and activities that don't involve death."

"Okay," I said, trying to smile brightly, feeling my face stretch all the wrong ways as I did.

Rob reached across the table and cupped my chin. "You're going to think I have forgotten her, and I haven't," he said. "Okay. We'll take a little look around. Remember, we don't want to take any risks."

I knew, though, and so did Rob, how long two minutes could be.

At least, I thought I knew.

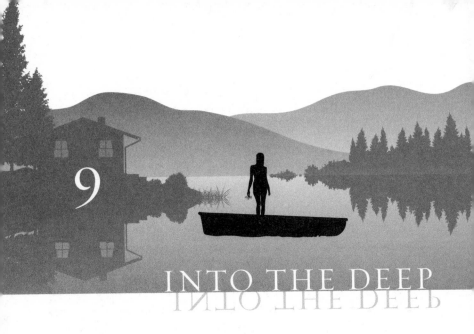

9

INTO THE DEEP

INTO THE DEEP

In a sturdy little inflatable Odyssey dive boat that probably folded up to the size of a can of tuna, with a motor that probably ran on vegetable oil, Wesley motored us out to the spot he remembered. Sure enough, his big headlamp picked up a reflector buoy instantly. Rob's map was only insurance . . .

It was cold, and I'd slipped on my parka and fingerless gloves. This was skiing weather, although everyone was complaining about the absence of snow and hoping it would show up for Christmas Eve in a few days. Going *into the water* in this weather defied all logic. To pass the moments, I asked Wesley, "What was your best dive ever?"

Without hesitation: "South America. Flooded Mayan ruins of burial caves."

"Were there still skulls?" I asked.

Rob shot me a look.

"There were still whole people, skeletonized of course, in these beautifully woven baskets as long as a regular coffin,"

Wesley said. "Some of those burials were thousands of years old. Big and little. The care given was very moving. Some of the coffins were decorated with masks and long braids of shells and beads."

"How did they not float away?"

"There were woven nets."

So if Tabor really had disappeared down the door in the ground to the old boathouse, then the evidence might still be there. He would have devised some way to keep them in place, to make it easy to revisit. As Wesley cut the motor, I looked up at the lights of the Tabor Oaks, where Garrett Tabor lived now—where I had first seen him in the empty penthouse with that poor girl. This was where old Dr. Simon Tabor took his sons, Dr. Andrew and Garrett's father, Stephen, to play fifty years ago, when the foundations where the Tabor Oaks once stood had been the family's summer cottages. Here was where they learned to sail and to fish. There was a sand bar where the kids probably swam, and then the water dropped off. That was where they'd sunk the boat. As we patted ourselves down and slipped out of our parkas, I thought: *How would I feel?*

What if I actually found a person? Would I forget everything and suck in the whole lake?

Wesley dropped the anchor and slipped into the water in his thick dry suit. I envied him his warmth. We had agreed that he'd stop when Rob and I were two-thirds of the way down. He'd let us go by ourselves to maximize the independence of our experience of the dive. The moon was high and the water in the cover as still and dark as tea.

After buckling on my weights and carefully fitting my dive boots into my fins, I banished all thoughts of the ferocity of the deep. Lake Superior, I told myself, was like New York

City: a giant place of small neighborhoods. This neighbor-hood was a just a corner: it had a small grocery and . . . and a flower shop and a used bookstore. It would be fine. Although it wasn't embraceable, like Ghost Lake or The Little Caul-dron, it was friendly. Wesley dropped his anchor as Rob and I clung to the side of the little inflatable.

"Are you ready, honey?" Rob said, snapping his tiny Glad-iator underwater camera to the outside of his weight belt.

"As I'll ever be," I said, meaning that.

We put on our masks and snorkels—and after one last good breath, we dropped away, supple as dolphins. Suddenly I felt good. Rob could be right. This was just a Rob-and-Allie adventure, a Christmas treat. Down we went, carefully adjusting the pressure in our ears, meeting Wesley in a circle of brightness to give him the high sign. Then we dropped more, ten feet, and another ten. I glanced at my watch. Just thirty-five seconds.

Rob began snapping photos of the glorious nursery for lake wildlife, sunnies and pike and the promised sturgeon, as long as my body and as big around as my waist. We dared to glide past the boat wreck to the caves under the cliff. It was harder then—water dark as hematite. It was hard not to think. But I didn't think. I let my eyes take the place of my mind, reaching up to switch my headlamp to the next higher beam, only dimly aware of the growing urge to breathe. I pointed to the pilings that must once have formed the foundation of the Tabors' old boathouse. Rob snapped a picture of me. Then, what looked like smears of dark paint were the natural mouths of caves in the cliffs. I moved gently in front of Rob, into the opening of one of the larger ones, half made of natural stone, half capped with a sort of little cornice that had once been an old brick window opening or something. I could feel from my lungs that we were closing in on ninety seconds. There wasn't much time left.

The caves were filled with other creatures: moon-bright spiders and striders, fish quick and pale as needles. A moment later, with Rob close behind me, I came to a man-made wall, the remnant of a concrete structure, not the back of the cave. To the right, there was a lake-born corridor. I turned to glance down it, knowing I would have to turn back fast and soon begin our ascent.

Immediately, I glimpsed the dull glow of something that wasn't natural. It was man-made metal: a chain, a big, thick chain, of the kind people used to secure boats.

There was a link and some bright, floating thread.

I pulled the chain and it slipped in space toward me. At the end of the chain was an object. The long, bright floating thread thickened and spread, around her forehead, marbled and blue, threads of skin, an expanse of bone, great holes where eyes had been, but teeth, still perfect, parted in a cry.

10

CAVE DWELLERS

CAVE DWELLERS

Everything happened so fast then.

While I would never be able to forget the next thirty seconds, I would never really be able to remember them, either.

When I saw the first skull, my Allie-mind came roaring back into my free-dive consciousness, and I almost exhaled. From the small explosions of pin lights bursting beside me, I could tell Rob was taking pictures. He was right there with me, witnessing everything I was witnessing. Tears spurted from the corners of my eyes behind my mask.

So close now.

Keep it together.

I could not lose it.

Think of nothing.

But you can't go back to thinking of nothing, from thinking of something.

I will not lose it, I thought.

That is the best way to lose it.

I will end up down here with them forever because I'll blow a circuit in my brain.

But I didn't. I summoned the person my mother calls "Alexis," my given name—whom I have come to think of as the child I once was or the woman I would be. Knowing that Rob was capturing this on film, and that we were both fully present, I was bursting with the need to breathe but able to hold it off just for a few seconds more. I let myself think: *Here it is. This is the proof you wanted. This is what Garrett Tabor hid. He did not want you to find it, or maybe he did want you to find it. This is why Juliet died. She knew all this. You must know it, too.*

I looked.

Ten seconds can be a long time. It can be long enough.

There were four girls chained to the wall. Remnants of clothing clung to delicate arms still articulated, wrist to elbow, young shoulder to bony breast. They swept their rags from side to side like finery as they twisted and turned in their shackles. In my centered brain, they appeared to be dolls dancing, or puppets trying to cast off their strings. Rob tapped me from behind. There was no way he could squeeze in next to me. I would need to back out, or turn and exit, to make way for him.

Once in a while, I thought of the extraordinarily sane-beyond-her-years self every chronically sick kid is supposed to be as Alexis Lin Kim. I thought of my ordinary self as Allie.

Alexis, I thought. *Stop. Stop, Alexis. In your life, you will touch dead people, not as a pathologist would, but as an evidence technician would. You will be around them. You promised to let them tell you their secrets. Like these girls, those dead people will be in chains—if not real chains, then the chains of circumstance. They need you to speak for them, because they can't speak anymore. They need you to find the marks and cuts and bits of tissue and material that will tell the stories they would tell.*

Remembering my own self just little more than a month ago, sitting in the car screaming after I had stolen the poncho, I recognized that girl again: here tonight, almost as though I could reach out and put my arms around her. Alexis Lin Kim said to poor Allie, "I know, this sucks."

The pictures would be enough to prove everything. Anything I touched would be ruined. That's the first rule of . . . well, anything, from crime to archaeology.

But then I saw it.

On the bobbing neck of the first girl—the one with the long, long blonde tassels of hair, knotted somehow, like dreadlocks—I caught a hint of something that gleamed in the beam of my headlamp.

It was a delicate necklace with a little charm.

The chain still held by the slimmest thread. It had been driven through a piece of what looked like some sort of red wool fabric, once maybe a sweater. Every current seemed to beg it away. So I reached out and tugged, and when it came loose, I glanced down at it. The charm was embossed with a hieroglyph or symbol fashioned out of gold. There was a muted sound. When I looked up, I almost screamed.

Her forehead tapped my facemask. We were so close to each other we could have kissed.

Another girl had slipped forward.

Five.

Dark-haired and fair, this one, oh no, oh hell, she still had skin, porous and pink as a baby's bath sponge. The swell of the water tipped her chin up.

Where her eyes were, there were crabs.

Alexis Lin Kim, be calm! screamed my head.

No, said Allie.

I had to go. I had to go right then.

Turning to Rob, and signaling my intention, I began to kick for the surface. He didn't follow. Impossible. I could not be seeing Rob, limp, unresponsive, hanging in the water like a coat on a pole.

But that was what I was seeing. Rob was in fact sinking, deeper, the twenty additional feet toward the lake bottom.

Forcing myself to ignore the need to breathe was like running back into a burning house. I reversed my direction, grabbed Rob, and—holding him with the fabric of his hood bunched in my fist—began to pull both of us toward the surface. There was the cord, the anchor cord that would lead to Wesley.

Shoving the little pendant inside my sleeve, I freed a hand. My lungs were coals, my brain firing fragmented fireworks. I pulled on the cord. I pulled again.

In the eternity of a single second it took for me to kick my way up to Wesley and for him to climb his way down to me, I tried not to think how heavy and inert Rob felt. I glanced at his face. His lips were dark. I drew back and kneed Rob in the chest.

Then, Wesley was forcing his buddy regulator between Rob's lips, sharing his own regulator with me, as we all hung, like fish on a stringer, along the braided yellow nylon lifeline, gulping air, inflating ourselves with sustaining oxygen. Rob's eyes fluttered, and he began to wrestle his way out of Wesley's grasp. He was bullishly strong and horribly pale. In that instant, nothing mattered but that he was alive.

I would have risked my life for him.

My mother was right.

I had risked my life for him.

Disoriented, probably not knowing at all where he was, Rob began to flail side to side, more powerful than either Wesley or me. As he thrashed in this silent-movie shot in the dark water, he opened his hand. I saw something slip from his glove, and I opened my mouth in a silent roar of protest. It was Rob's little Gladiator: the camera that had captured the truth, tumbling away to the floor of the lake. I turned my headlamp down but could not catch sight of it. I was in no condition to attempt another free dive, but how could I let it get away? I prepared to take another breath and then go down after it.

Wesley held me firmly. He nudged me, urgently pointing toward the surface. More than anything, we needed to get Rob to help.

When we broke through, I gasped for breath. Rob remained conscious. In spite of everything, I was close to calm. *Rob is alive.* Wesley let down the ladder, and we all heaved into the little Odyssey.

"What happened?" Wesley said once he'd fired up and was zipping back toward the beach. I'd never seen him so rattled. "Did Rob faint? I don't scare easy, but a DWB is usually lethal. I'm glad you were with him, and you kept your head."

Trust Wesley to use some outdoorsy acronym at a time like this.

"I don't know," I managed between gulps of air. "We went to the mouth of the one of the caves in the cliff, behind the ruins of the sunken boats and the boat house. And Wesley, down there, we saw . . ." Rob moaned and grabbed my hand. "Are you okay, honey? Does it hurt anywhere?"

Rob made a throat-cutting motion and pointed up at the

rapidly approaching windows of the Tabor Oaks. Several of
the condominiums had lavishly trimmed trees on the balconies. They stood up hale and brave, like the stout little blue
spruce Angie and I had decorated last week for our own living room—a place I wished I were right now. Some of the
sliding doors up there were framed in twinkle lights, and a
belt of red fairy lights went around the roof, where Juliet,
Rob, and I had stood once, so long ago.

He lived there.

Garrett Tabor was near.

He was near to his harem of dead brides.

Near me.

He may have lived in the apartment where the Cryers
used to live, the place where I babysat for a few months.
Although Dr. Stephen owned the building and he would
have painted and cleaned, nothing is ever really, really
gone, so Garrett Tabor's molecules rubbed against my own
every day. Except for the penthouse, which—I now saw as
I glanced up—had been for sale. The Cryers' was the only
vacant place in the building. Garrett Tabor would have had
no need of a four-bedroom penthouse. He had to live there.
That's what Rob meant.

While I was supposedly the intuitive one, Rob got something that I hadn't understood until now. A chill that had
nothing to do with the icy wind and my freezing wet suit
crept down past my tongue and swallowed my words, along
with the iron tang of lake water.

Wesley had unzipped Rob's suit, pulling off the top portion, and had laid two of the warm blankets he'd brought in a
thermal bag over Rob's shoulders. I struggled out of my own
wet suit and, shivering, huddled in one of the blankets and
pulled a stocking cap over my head.

Wesley had his gloves off and his phone out of his water-proof gear bag. "It's only eleven, and he's probably put in a full day with the ski team, but he'll get up. Yep. There's the light." I heard the muffled sound of a voice on Wesley's phone. "Gary! Hey, man, it's Wesley Krauss. To you, too, buddy, but here's the thing. I'm approaching the beach down west of your parking lot in a rubber Odyssey with two free divers, kids. Yes. Rob Dorn and Allie . . . yes, Allie. Sure, you know them. I have been training them. Rob had an incident out there. No, he absolutely is completely conscious, no signs of that I can see . . . Okay. That's great, man. About one minute out."

Turning to us, Wesley explained that Gary Tabor was summoning an ambulance and would do "triage" himself—was even now, healer that he was, grabbing more blankets, a thermos of warm fluid, and a blood pressure cuff.

I blinked at Wesley. Of course he would have called "Gary." That was the logical thing to do. I felt sick in the same way as when I'd encountered "Gary" at the morgue.

"Rob," I called over the sound of the motor and the water. "Are you okay?" Weakly, he gave me the thumbs-up sign. I leaned close to his ear. "Did you see them? Did you see the chains? Did you see the bodies?"

I knew from Rob's eyes when he opened them wide and his mouth formed an uncomprehending gape, he didn't see a thing. It was not possible, but I was still alone.

As we smacked into the spit of beach, the velocity of the wind hit, and an ambulance and fire truck peeled into the parking lot. Lights flipped on in the condominiums; fire-fighters called up assurances that this was an accident, that all was well, there was no fire. The paramedics lifted Rob out of the Odyssey. Laying him gently on a flexible stretcher, they trotted for the open bay doors of the ambulance, and tugging off my fins, I ran across the pebbled, cold sand after him. Garrett Tabor appeared around the edge of one of the open doors.

"You got this?" he said, as though he was one of the medics.

"We're good."

"Hi, Allie," he said. "Always an adventure, huh?"

I said nothing. Wesley and Garrett Tabor bro-hugged, and Wesley helped me out of my wet suit and held up a rubber sheet while I slipped out of my bathing suit and into the warm sweats I'd packed. The thought of Garrett Tabor on the other side of an envelope-thick bit of rubber, the only material that separated him from my naked body, caught me in the gut. I leaned on Wesley and vomited hot sour nothing in the sand.

"Let me look at her," Tabor said, approaching me with his stethoscope.

I screamed. "No!"

Wesley said, "She's just freaked out, man."

Tabor backed off, palms outward. "It's okay, Allie."

I reached up to turn off my miner's light before pulling off my hood, as Wesley shook out my wet suit.

We saw it fall at the same moment, like a golden tear against the pale sand. The little pendant on its broken chain fell from the sleeve of my wet suit. If you didn't know Garrett Tabor for what he was, you would not have seen the lurch of his shoulders, the involuntary near-lunge to snatch up the prize he so clearly recognized. But I went first. With nothing to fear except everything, I reached down and closed my cold hand around its cold surface, slipping it into the zipped hip pocket of my sweats.

No one can save me now, I thought.

And then I looked up at Tabor's eager, so-false grin.

I thought, *Bring it, you piece of shit. I'll go down, but I'll take you, too.*

11

CRACKS IN THE ICE

CRACKS IN THE ICE

Rob spent the night at the hospital, being treated for hypothermia and exposure. It was more or less an excuse to keep him there, to make sure nothing else was wrong, because he was basically unhurt. He'd coughed up what little water was in his lungs, and he'd only briefly lost consciousness.

My mother was already at the hospital. As the nurse in charge of PM's at the emergency room, she monitored the radio. She was just ending her shift when she heard—for about the fifth time in six months—that the incoming guests were part of her own crew.

So she waited. We got there about 11:20 P.M., and my mother had probably reached the point of no return, anger-wise, maybe fifteen minutes earlier after transmissions from the paramedics made it clear that I was alive and well.

When Jackie strode into the cubicle where I was waiting with Rob and Wesley, her posture was about as yielding and maternal as a sawed-off shotgun. She gave me a quick once-over, and said, "We'll deal with this privately."

Whenever my mother said she wanted to deal with anything privately, I wanted our next encounter to take place in an airport or a federal building, because nothing, nothing, could go well if she got me alone and went savage. With very clear exceptions that were compulsory given her overprotective nature, Jackie likes to think of herself as nurturing my independence. She's more or less in favor of every nutty thing I do. She wants me to feel and be free, despite wishing she could wear me like a lapel pin to make sure that I don't do anything at all.

I had thought that she would freak out about Parkour; instead, she had said it was beautiful. She never took that back, even after Juliet disappeared. What she would think about my going deep into dark, cold water that would have frozen if it didn't have wave action, without an air source, I could only imagine. I really didn't want to imagine.

So when my mom stalked out, telling me to go ahead and stay with Rob, that she was going to call her best friend Gina and *go get a drink* when it was *nearly midnight*—which was the equivalent of my mother of telling me she was going to meet her drug connection and score a few rocks of cocaine, I had two reactions. The first: I hoped Gina would talk her down, murmuring things about kids and look what we did when we were young . . . and my trembling increased. Because my second reaction was picturing myself forced to withdraw from John Jay and work at the hot pretzel stand in the lobby of the Timbers Ski Resort at night for a semester, until I learned a lesson.

When Rob's parents showed up at the hospital, we were both busted again.

If only Wesley had been able to keep his mouth shut. But, Wesley was the moral equivalent of an Eagle Scout, and he spilled everything about our recent hobby, down to the risks of a DWB.

For this Mrs. Dorn decided to blame me.

Ignoring me, she said to Rob, fuming, "Don't you have enough problems without going for a little dip in a freezing lake, especially without an oxygen tank?"

Weakly, Rob protested that Wesley was there, and that we were never at any real risk.

"Risk?" Mrs. Dorn said. "Risk is all you do. You and her. Isn't it enough that Juliet is dead? Doesn't that make you want to think about the time you have and—"

"It's all the more reason," Rob said, struggling to sit up. He did look weak and ashy. I was proud of him, but I sort of wanted him to take it easy.

Mrs. Dorn started to cry, and Mr. Dorn, whom I'd never seen do anything but smile, frowned at Rob. "Why do you want to go and worry her?" he said.

"Obviously I didn't want to worry her or I would have told you guys about it," Rob said.

This is actual logic, but it does not cut ice with parents, ever.

The ER doctor, Brice or Brick or one of the other guys about five years older than me whom my mother flirted with, told the Dorns he was admitting Rob. They all turned and looked at me like I was some kind of infected bug bite. I shrugged. It was ten degrees outside. My mother was out at a tavern. What was I supposed to do, walk home? Half-heartedly, Mr. Dorn said I could drive Rob's car and return it tomorrow night, but Rob's car was parked back at the Tabor Oaks and I would rather have spent the night on a plastic couch in the lobby than go back there to pick it up.

Wesley said then, "No hassle, parents. I went to school

with one of the medics and they'll give me a ride to my car. I'll take Allie home."

It was all so stiff and awkward that I didn't even kiss Rob goodbye.

"THAT WAS ONE tense moment," Wesley said after we'd been ferried by ambulance to his car, parked behind the Y. It had to be one of the first Volkswagens ever made, and the floor was not made of floor, but of some kind of pasteboard, like cheap bookshelves. It also had no radio, no heat, and seatbelts that looked like the kind that you see in old movies about airplane crashes. "I don't mean the hospital. I meant out there on the lake. It doesn't mean Rob should give up free diving though. That happens even to the best."

Thanking Wesley for his kindness, I rushed inside my house, now feeling that frozen-through way you do when you are certain you will never be warm again. As I opened the double locks with my keys, my phone pinged.

Good.

Rob was telling me he loved me and his parents had calmed down.

As I opened the door, I fished my phone out of my front pack.

UNKNOWN had texted: You have something that belongs to me.

The door opened the rest of the way, and I nearly fell in.

"I don't need a babysitter," Angela complained. She was looking up at me, wearing pajamas with moose on them that were about two sizes too big for her frame, which went about fifty pounds soaking wet.

The phone pinged again.

Leave it in my inbox at the lab, in a sealed envelope, and we'll pretend this never happened.

Pretend this never happened? I was ready to call the Navy Seals to go down there tonight and rescue those girls—not their lives, but their justice—and secure Garrett Tabor's comeuppance. Even though Rob had dropped the camera, the camera was down there, somewhere, although the thought of the restless ebb of Superior's waters made me wary about how far it could tumble before anyone could get back to it. Still, the girls were there. I'd seen them. Rob might have seen them, too, and that was why he panicked. Maybe he remembered by now, having shaken off his stupor.

Pretend this never happened?

I had Tabor. I *had* him.

It was just a matter of who to call first. I had to think things through. If I called the nearest regional office of the FBI before calling the local police, there would be delays and all kinds of official weirdness. If I called the local police, well . . . my record of luck with calling the local police was the strongest possible disincentive.

"Did you even hear me?" Angie said.

Distracted, I answered, "Well, you might not need a babysitter. I would like someone to make me bagel pizzas and play the kind of Monopoly with me where you don't just go around the board, but you get to buy all the properties and make loans and stuff. How come you don't want that?"

I paid the babysitter, Mrs. Staples, and exchanged the look you give adults that says, *Kids, huh . . .* Even if you don't mean it. All the while I was thinking, who can I call? What the hell am I going to do? Do they put heinous-crime discovery off for the holidays? It was three days before Christmas Eve. My grandmother would be coming, and my Uncle Brian, with his wife and their two daughters.

As Mrs. Staples closed the door, Angela went on complaining, "If I did need a babysitter, I wouldn't want it to be her. She reads me parts from her books, and they creep me out. She says, 'How's this, Ange?' I hate it when people call me Ange. She reads me things like, 'He clutched her back, where the heat of her skin burned through the thin wisp of silk . . .' Why do I want to hear that? I'm nine."

I pulled Angela down onto my lap and patted her hair, still bowling options around in my mind. To my mother's horror, Angela and her friend Keely had recently decided to razor-cut their hair, employing blades they pried from disposable ladies' shavers. Keely looked like a baby chicken. Nobody could do anything to make Angela's thick, blue-black hair—shiny as ice—look anything but pretty. This had come close. With her big tip-tilted eyes, she looked like an anime character.

"I think it's nice that she respects your opinion, Angela. That's what people have to hear when they're too old for a babysitter," I said. "And since when is . . . you just said you're nine! Third graders have babysitters."

Angela pouted. Mrs. Staples's romance novels, published directly to ebooks under the name Roxanne Royale, were brisk sellers. She finished a new one every two weeks, and some people said she sold more than fifty thousand copies of the last one.

What was *she* still doing in Iron Harbor?

What was I?

"Could you eat?" I asked Angela. Stuffing my face helped me think.

I made sandwiches of roast beef, cheese, tomatoes, lettuce, Thousand Island dressing, mayonnaise, and pickles. Angela ate hers and a quarter of mine. I made another one for me.

"Can we make ice cream?" she said.

"No."

One of the both ridiculously expensive and fetching things my Grandma Mack had given us last Christmas was an ice-cream maker that produced soft serve in fifteen minutes. As it was getting near to Christmas, my mother had to inventory the storage spaces and get out all the things her mother had bought that we'd never used. She placed them on the counter tops so they'd look as though we used them daily.

"It only takes fifteen minutes," Angie said. "*Fifteen* minutes."

She would keep on needling me for thirty, so I got out a bag of frozen blueberries and my mother's one concession to food hedonism: half and half.

In fifteen minutes, we had gooey, (and I have to admit) delicious blueberry ice cream.

Angie said she couldn't sleep unless we watched scary movies. Although I had done this to her, I pleaded, "Hey Angie, it's nearly one in the morning."

And where was my mother? With Brice or Court or Haven or some other intern with a post-her-generation name?

"Part?" Angie said. "Of one?"

I needed to think, so I agreed.

We popped in a classic, *Night of the Living Dead*. She was out in fewer than twenty minutes. So like me was my Angie now that what would have kept another nine-and-a-half-year-old up all night expecting zombies to rip off the shutters sent my sister to sleep after half an hour. I carried her in to my queen-sized bed, so if she woke up she would feel special—and sure that zombies could not get her there, if she were to feel afraid at all. Even though I wouldn't be there with her until just before she got up, I knew that Angie still loved to wake up in my bed, sick with ultra-stuffed pillows and the most lavish sheets my mom could find, about twelve hundred-count sheets. Angela said that the scent of the lavender I used to spray my sheets and pillows felt like a hug to her.

I was about to leave the room when on a whim, I decided to lie down next to her. Even unconscious, Angela did her own sleep ritual, burrowing into the quilts and twisting one around her like the cotton candy twists around the paper cone.

Then, in the dark—no room is darker than mine; it's like the inside of your favorite pillow—Angela suddenly woke. She said, "Allie?"

"Hmmm."

"If Juliet was a zombie, would she kill me?"

"There are no zombies," I said. "And if Juliet were here, she would climb in bed with you and tickle you. She would be so happy to be with you again. She loved you, Angela."

"Could there be a good zombie?"

"I don't think so."

"Are there zombie angels?"

I hugged Angela. *Zombie angels.* Juliet would have dug the image. It would have appealed to the twisted side of her nature.

"Go to sleep now, my little zombie girl," I said.

I was about to get up and clean the kitchen (as well as the living room, the loft, and possibly the garage for extra points) when I heard the door open.

Rather, it *banged* open, smacking the plaster so hard that there'd be a dent.

My first thought was that it was Garrett Tabor, that he had somehow defeated our multiple locks and our security system, too.

It was, however, my mother, and she did not look in the least tipsy. She looked about twice her size, like one of those fish that can puff itself out. Gina was behind her.

"Hi, Gina," I said. "Hey, Mom. Glad you're here. Angie's asleep. I have to do some reading so . . ."

"You sit down right there," Jackie said. "Do. Not. Move."

Gina retreated. I couldn't believe it. She was going to leave me there to the wrath of Jacqueline Mack Kim. I made an imploring gesture. Gina pretended that she thought I was only waving, and she waved back.

Chicken.

Gina gently closed the door, her lips forming a kiss.

Traitor.

"I have been tolerant. I have been supportive. I have been all the things that mothers should be. Have I done that? Have I?"

"You have, Jack-Jack," I said, feebly.

"Don't even try horsing around with me. Don't even try. It's not enough that I have spent nearly eighteen years worried about my very loved child. Is it? It's not enough that your best friend, who was also like my child, just died. You have to go sink yourself in lake water the temperature of cold beer. And why? Why now? Why not in summer? Why in December?" She paused, and slammed her palm flat against the granite countertop. "Here's a better question. Why at all?"

"Free diving is actually easier in the . . ." I remembered Jackie's favorite phrase. "It's biology. The mammalian diving reflex . . ."

"I don't care! This is unacceptable, Alexis. For what, Alexis? For what?"

"Because I know what he did."

"Who?"

"Garrettt Tabor. I know . . . Mom, sit down."

She did.

My phone, between us on the counter top, began to ping. I snatched it up, hiding the screen from my mother. Texts were arriving. They were photos. The first one was of my mother and Gina, exchanging a hug. It couldn't have been more than five minutes earlier. The second was . . . it was Angela. Dressed in her snowmobile suit, using a broom to knock snow out of the trees where our backyard opened onto a portion of the Superior National Hiking Trail. Angela's snowmobile suit was only a week old. That picture would have had to have been taken by someone with a long lens . . . or standing in our driveway, observing my sister unawares. There were more. Angela with Keely at the bus stop. Angela walking into school. My mother and Gina on a run in their woolies and headbands. In all, there were a dozen pictures.

He didn't have to tell me that he could get close to the people closest to me.

He could get way too close.

All it would take would be a wheel over a curb on a dark morning, a car that came out of nowhere. Tabor knew how to do that. I had surgical pins in my arm to prove it.

How did he know that we were talking, here . . . now?

Shoving my phone in the front pocket of my big hoodie, I jumped to my feet and yanked the kitchen blinds down so hard that they jangled crooked on their tracks.

Was he watching us now?

"What's wrong with you?" Jackie asked.

"We were watching a horror movie. Angela and I were. The girl looked up and there was this creepy burned guy with this face pressed up to the window. I just looked out there, and it was so black and cold." I thought of that night on the balcony of the Tabor Oaks, and Tabor's face as he calmly looked at me. His handsome face, worse than any distorted rubber monster mask. My life was a horror movie. "Mom, I'm sorry. I have to prove to myself," I said, improvising desperately. "I have to prove that I can go on without her, Mom. I have to prove that whatever Garrett Tabor and Juliet did together has nothing to do with me now. Maybe it wasn't a great idea for us to try free diving now. But I'm grieving now. And I'm lonely now. And so is Rob."

Don't believe me, I thought. *What I'm saying sounds nuts. Call me on it. I would collapse and just tell you.*

"What did Rob want?" my mother asked.

I had no idea what she meant. Then I realized she believed that the cascade of texts had come from Rob.

"I ask for a reason," she added. "You're not going anywhere tonight."

"I won't see Rob that much over Christmas . . ."

"You should have considered that before. It seems that for the past year, all you've done is risk your life in stupid ways." Jackie got up, as well, and she got in my face, close to me. She had never spanked me or even given me a slap on the butt when I was a child. At this moment, it wasn't out of the question that she would slug me. She was breathing hard. Her hair was sticking up like she'd tried to craft a faux-hawk for Halloween. "When is your birthday, Alexis?"

"That would be January eighteenth," I said. "You were there, remember?"

Jackie grabbed my arm. "I don't care how old you are. The day you turn eighteen is the next time you leave this house except for work. And I will drive you to work. Do you hear me? Do you?"

"I hear you," I said. "I'm sorry." For the first time since I was ten, I crossed my fingers behind my back. Now, I would have to evade not only the authorities, but Garrett Tabor and my mother to prove what I had seen. I would do it, though. I would do it somehow.

12

BREAKING UP

BREAKING UP

The next night, I asked Rob to buy me a camera. We were sitting alone, side by side on my bed, in the dark, music quietly playing from my dock.

"For your birthday?" he said. "I sort of had a plan for that, actually."

"Well, I was thinking before. I was thinking for nothing. I've never asked anybody for anything in my life, like since I was little and wanted a Dracula's Daughter doll. But I need a camera better than mine. I need a camera that does better video than mine." I stopped and took his hand. "But that a dummy person like me could use."

"No offense, Allie-Stair, but why are you asking me to buy you a camera? I don't mean I won't. I just wonder why, because you have money. I mean, I know you have enough that even if you didn't have savings, if it was for school or something, then Jackie would . . ." Rob turned over in the darkness and drew me close, throwing his leg over mine.

"Jackie can't know. That's why. If I buy anything online,

she'll know. Since we dived, since you got hurt or in danger because of me, I'm officially her ex-kid."

"I get that. It could have been you. She was scared."

"Her scared is over and she's furious."

"Well, maybe now. But not for long. That's bullshit. It's two days until Christmas Eve. She's not going to stay mad at you over Christmas, Allie."

"Believe me, she is."

Rob knew my mom well, but he didn't know the kind of anger engendered by the thought of her daughter beating XP only to drown. My mother would be civil to me in front of our relatives, for the week between Christmas and New Year's Eve, when my Grandma Mack paid for the whole family (including Mom, Angie, and me) to stay up at The Timbers on Torch Mountain in a big chalet, to ski every night (and every day, for everyone else).

"It won't get here in time for Christmas," Rob said. "The camera."

I nodded, biting back tears. Christmas this year was a difficult subject between us.

Rob was going skiing, too. He was going skiing in Vail with his parents, leaving in one day. When my Uncle Brian arrived in Duluth, Rob would be taking off at the same airport. We weren't married, or engaged, or anything. But it felt wrong for us to spend Christmas apart the first Christmas after Juliet's death, the first Christmas that we were a couple. Still, we were kids, and there was no way that we could buck our parents' wishes. The Dorns thought they were giving Rob a treat—he'd always wanted to ski Vail or Mammoth or Whistler—but I suspected also that, especially now, they didn't particularly want him around me.

"We can wait until after Christmas," I said.

"It could be after New Year's."

"Well, it'll come before then, and I can do this myself."

"What do you want to do yourself, Allie?"

"I don't want to tell you."

"Allie, since when do we have secrets?"

"Not ever." But we had, and we did.

"Then tell me."

We had agreed that I had mental problems where it came to Garrett Tabor. Why should I reinforce this already unfounded, unfair idea by telling . . . the truth?

But this was Rob. So I blurted out, "I want to take video of him . . . like surveillance. I want to set the camera up on a timer so that it would take a few minutes every hour, so I can see what he does when he comes and goes. I could see what he carries with him. I want to take pictures so I can remember exactly where we saw the bodies . . ."

Rob sat there motionless.

"You saw them. You saw the skeletons."

Rob said nothing.

"You saw them!" Just as it was impossible that Rob had nearly died down there, it was impossible, for *the third time*, that he had failed to see what I saw. It could not have happened. He hadn't seen the dead girl in the apartment, the second time we scaled the Tabor Oaks. He hadn't seen Juliet with Garrett Tabor at the Fire Festival.

"You were taking pictures!" I said, grabbing for his shirt, not to hurt him, not to startle him, but to shake him—to make him remember. "You dropped the camera, Rob, but the camera has pictures of them. I saw the flash going off."

Rob's voice was muffled. I imagined him covering his face with his big hands. "I don't even remember taking pictures, Allie. I passed out. All I remember is waking up in the hospital. I've tried, honey. I don't even remember being in the boat. I don't remember seeing Tabor at all."

"So, you think I made it up. Anyone would think I made it up. Skeleton girls chained to the old pillars, pushed back inside the cliff cave. It sounds like a horror movie. Maybe I'll only be able to find the place that once. So he gets away again." I started to cry. "Then where did I get the chain? Where did I get the medal?"

That I still hadn't shown Rob. That I hadn't figured out. I could feel it in my drawer, glowing and pulsing as though it had its own small power source, a beacon that that had led me to it. I struggled to pull myself together. This would be our last night for ten days. "It's not your fault. It's not your fault, Rob. I'm sorry that I'm making it feel like your fault."

"I know you're not trying to, but I do feel that way."

"No, no . . ." Roughly, I wiped the tears off my cheeks and chin and steadied my voice. "Let's forget it. Let's forget it for tonight. Those . . . bodies, if that's what they were, have been there for years. They're not going anywhere."

Rob got up and stood with his hands pressed against the frame of my big bedroom window. "You can't forget it, Allie."

Without another word, Rob sat down at my computer. I saw my screen come to life. He punched in a website and ordered me a Canon G12 with an extra lens, a bag, a sturdy tripod, an underwater case, and a weather housing. I saw him charge it and I glimpsed the price, with a sharp, involuntary gasp. It was more than six hundred bucks of camera and equipment—with being on deep sale for the holidays.

"It will be here tomorrow," he said dully. "It's just like one of mine. It takes great video."

"Rob . . . you didn't need to do that now . . ."

"Well, sure. I did. I won't be here to help you. And I'm not sure that I would want to help you if I was going to be here."

I stood to reach for him, and then stopped. "Well, tonight we'll feast! I'm going to make shrimp curry for us. Surprise!" It's the one thing I'm really good at cooking—curry. I try to save it for special occasions. "I got all the stuff yesterday."

Rob murmured that he wasn't up for it.

"You love my curry." I flipped on the soft-glow burgundy shaded bedside lamp and sneaked my arms around his waist. Rob was unyielding, all angles and resistance.

"I love your curry, but I don't think I could keep it down tonight. Don't take it as though it's a personal thing."

"What's wrong with you?" I asked. "Did you inhale something toxic down there?"

"I was checked out."

"You don't look right. You look pale and tired."

He said, "I am pale and tired."

"Why?"

"Like you say, I keep meaning to lay down a good base tan but I never get around to it."

"You know what I mean. Are you sick?"

"I'm as well as I'm ever going to be."

"Rob!" I socked him on the bicep, hard, and was shocked when he winced. "Rob! Why would you say something so feeble?"

"Even if we have a normal lifespan, Allie. Even if we live to be eighty-six years old, you don't get to be healthier than you are when you're a guy who's seventeen, nearly eighteen. That's all I mean."

Apprehension wobbled through me.

"You're putting this in a weird way."

"All I mean is, I'm under a lot of stress."

"Why?"

"Well, we just found the burial ground of what, five girls and I don't even remember it . . ."

"Before that. You looked tired at Juliet's funeral. You looked tired even before."

"Allie-Stair! That's just dumb! I'd been up for three days. So why wouldn't I look tired? She was my best friend, too. Not like you, but I can't even say how horrible I feel about Juliet, or I'll cry like some asshole. You know, the last few months didn't just happen to you!"

"What about before? You were . . . skinny."

"I've always been skinny."

"Not like this."

"Like I said, I don't have a big appetite."

It was more than that, though, and both of us knew it. It was more than Juliet's death and the combined stresses of the past month. For the first time in weeks, I really saw Rob. I saw a guy who'd been slim and built who was now thin and anxious. Was I to blame for this? I was. I'd made him this way. I saw a guy who, like me, would always be X-tra Pale, who was now paper-white, the color of a petal on some night-blooming plant. I'd taken the bloom out of Rob's face. He didn't have to be this way. Terrified by a sign of weakness in him, I got angry. I marched out into the kitchen and assembled all of the ingredients for curry in a pot. Then, I set the table for one, with a cloth napkin and a candle, and proceeded to eat two helpings on my own.

Rob wanted cereal.

So I made him oatmeal with cinnamon, vanilla, raisins, and bad grace. It was a humiliating display of my worst self. I then came on to him stronger than I had since the first time we were together, basically pulling off his clothes in my room, even though Angela was at home and my mother was due back in an hour.

WE LAY TOGETHER then, in the dark, really together, holding each other. After what seemed like a very long time, while love that was far more than passion and youth flowed between us, the words that came to my mind were, my beloved friend. My Rob and only. Rob stood up and slipped into his clothes. Quietly, I did the same thing, combing out my messy hair with my fingertips.

Then, he reached in his jeans pocket and pulled something out, tossing it on the bed between us, a tiny, shiny package, unmistakably a box that had some kind of jewelry in it. "Open it, Allie. This was going to be your Christmas and birthday present. I'd like you to have it now." He held up his hand as I started to protest. "I would have given it to you now anyhow. I didn't picture it like this. I didn't think I was going to be ordered to go with my parents. But, I would like you to open it."

I slowly unwrapped the shiny, silvery paper, the texture of silk. The box was deep red velvet. I held my breath (I'd become gifted at doing this) and opened it. The ring was lovely, a simple, declarative, square-cut blue diamond flanked by two garnets. Garnet is my birthstone, the same as Rob's.

"Is this . . . what I think . . . ?"

"I guess. I had planned to take you out tonight, well, not out to a restaurant . . . but I bought catered food for us, at my place."

"You did?"

Where is it, I thought? Why aren't we there?

"And then?" I said.

"I was going to say, I love you, Allie. I've probably loved you all my life. And when we're out of school, or even when we're twenty, before we're out of school. I want to marry you."

I squeaked, "Really? You're proposing to me?" I jumped up off the bed and squeezed Rob hard around the neck. "Really? Yes. Yes. Yes. Yes!"

Slowly, without letting go of my hands, he unwound them from around his neck and then held them.

"Allie," he said. His voice was even and slow.

"I'm right here!"

"That is what I was *going* to do. I want you to have the ring. I designed it for you, specially. It will look beautiful on your hand."

Slowly, the implication slipped down over me like a cloak: I could have the ring, as a present. Rob wasn't telling me anything other than that it would be pretty on my hand.

"So you were going to do that, and what are you doing now?"

Rob said, "I don't know." Then he said the thing that no girl ever wants to hear her guy say. "I need time, Allie. I need time to think. Just a little time."

So it's over, I thought.

13

UNDIVIDED ME

UNDIVIDED ME

It was all I could do to get out of bed on Friday.

The two days since Rob and I parted were measured out in minutes, not hours. It was proof of the theory of relativity. When we were together, there was never enough time. Now, time was all I had. A hundred times, I picked up my phone to promise that I would stop my endless sleuthing obsession and try to be Rob-and-Allie-Before again.

But I knew that would be a lie. There was no Rob-and-Allie-Before anymore.

Slowly, I put my feet on the ground, and slowly, I pulled on a hefty black sweater that I felt I could huddle within, and with that, tights, and my fuzziest boots. Then I went through the little jewelry drawers in the top tier of my old bureau and dug up a long chain that would hang unobtrusively under my sweater. On it, I slipped Rob's ring and the little golden pendant. I wanted it close to me for proof. I guess I wanted the ring close to me for proof, too, that if Rob didn't love me anymore, he had once.

I wondered if Rob, on his way to Vail, picked up the phone, too. If he did, there was no sign of it.

I'd slept all day and most of the previous night. All I wanted to do was sleep, so that I could forget that one of the few things that made my life worth living was gone. Every time I thought about Rob, or took out one of his hoodies to inhale his warm laundry scent, I cried until I fell asleep again, only to wake a couple of hours later, with nothing different.

The idea of work that night was a relief. At least there would be something to distract me.

My mother drove me silently to the medical examiner's office. I know she suspected that something was wrong, but she was still in a foul mood, and hosting her older brother, Brian, always put her in a worse mood. Brian had the perfect life and the perfect family.

I hadn't decided what to tell Bonnie, or how much to involve her. Yet, I knew that she seemed to know a great deal about a wide variety of things, and I thought that, with her help, perhaps I could figure out what the pendant was . . . and then maybe I could figure out who the girl was that it had belonged to.

When Rob first saw it, he said, "It's some kind of symbol. Maybe it's Hebrew. Maybe it's Hindi."

Immediately, when he said that, I knew it wasn't.

"It's not," I said to him. "It's Chinese."

A memory of the first time I saw my little sister unfurled across my mind.

When we adopted Angela, I met my mother at the airport in Minneapolis with her brothers, Brian and Sean, and my grandmother. Mom had come all the way from a village south of Bejing with Angela, from Bejing to Chicago to Minneapolis. Angela had about five pairs of identical little black pajamas and two pairs of identical little slippers. On the one she was wearing, there was a little coin with a red cord pinned to the tunic. On the coin was Angela's lunar New Year symbol. She'd been born in the year of the dragon. There were also stamped characters that spelled out 'Kim." That had been her surname when she was born, or someone else's name entirely. It was impossible to keep it as her middle name because she would then have been Angela Kim Kim. Angela's dossier didn't even prove conclusively if the little pin came from the young woman who sadly had to abandon Angela literally on the doorstep of a church in Zhoukoudian—near the place where the so-called "Peking Man" and other ancient fossils were found. It might have been pinned on her by the nuns before she left for the United States, as a symbol of good luck.

The little golden pendant bore the same kind of symbol.

THAT NIGHT, BONNIE sought me out. She brought her son Chris to work with her; he was actually planning only on dropping her off on his way to go out. But he came in for a few moments. Everyone's fascinated by the morgue. Since I hadn't really gone to high school, I barely knew Chris, although he'd briefly dated Nicola Burns before Nicola died. He was the same age as I was, but still in high school, planning to go to DePaul in Chicago in the fall.

The lab was slow that night. Death takes holidays, too. I said to Chris, "Are you good with a computer search?"

He said, "Best in the West. I'm going to major in games design."

"Would you help me with some research?"

We spent an hour looking up Chinese characters for many different kinds of common words, but none of them looked

very much like the characters on the necklace. After she finished up a case she was working on, Bonnie came in.

"Maybe it's Japanese," Bonnie suggested.

We found it right away.

The little pendant spelled out the kata for the word *sora*,
which means *sky*.

"So. Now we basically know what it means. Would
that be someone's favorite thing?" Bonnie wondered aloud.
"Perhaps her hobby was astronomy?" She asked again who
the pendant belonged to. I told her that I didn't know, that
it was something we saw when we went free diving. All of
this was technically the truth.

Chris said, "Maybe it's a name."

"Sky?" I said. "No way."

"Not so fast," Bonnie said. "That's possible. Let me look
up this file I kept in Chicago." She went back to her own
computer.

"I went to grade school with a girl named Sunshine,"
Chris said. "People are always naming their kids things like
Destiny and Summer and stuff."

He was right, too, of course.

Together, we thought of the most outrageous names
in our combined experience: mine was limited. One of my
online work-study group partners for AP English was named
Theodora. One was a girl named Gus, short for Augusta,
and there was an older guy whose name was Hammersley.
Chris, like Rob, did online gaming, although Rob did it in
part because he could play all night long against people in all
kinds of time zones all over the world. One was named Tag-
gert, another Jonathan Johns, and there were brothers called
Dane and Shane. A player from Israel was named Uzi—the
gun is named after a person, not the other way around.

Bonnie found her informal computer file of horrible children's names; these were often inspired by the birth of twins, which apparently moved people to epic heights.

She recalled Sativa and Sensamilla, twin daughters of a young girl who apparently liked her weed.

"I'd bet every dollar I have that they've changed their names by now," Bonnie said. "Probably to Ann and Jane."

There were twins Dallas and Houston. Elegance and Eloquence. Hunter and Trapper. Imaboy and his sister, Imagirl. Precious and Patience. Rock and Star.

The singletons were just as awful.

Gracious Gal.

Cyborg.

Raven.

Kale.

I said, "That's a vegetable, right?" Bonnie nodded and kept on reading, swearing us to secrecy forever as she did.

Euclid.

Grasshopper.

Bus Stop Number Nineteen.

"You're making that up!" I said.

"That has got to be commemorative name," Chris said. "Like Bathroom Floor, Holiday Inn." I liked Chris. For a few minutes, because he was funny, I forgot that I was mourning. It was actually refreshing to have a friend. Bonnie kept clicking, egging us on. She showed us Camaro. Champ. Mercury. Passionette. Serendipity. Sherlock and Watson.

"That last one is too twisted," Chris said, cracking up. "Think about those kids!"

"Maybe their mom walked into the wrong movie," I said.

We hadn't heard the outer door open and close. We

looked up, and Garrett Tabor was standing in the door of the big office.

He said nothing. We said nothing. But I could hear my breath begin to come in gasps, ragged and loud as a dog's.

Bonnie crossed to the printer and removed the page that showed the Japanese characters that matched the necklace. Without looking down, I closed my hand over the pendant and slid it on to my lap.

How long had he been there?

"Let's get to work," Bonnie said. "Chris, I want to show you something interesting."

"Mom, I'm totaled. I'm going home," Chris told his mother. "Nice to see you, Allie. Hi, Coach."

Garrett Tabor nodded. Chris' younger brother—Bonnie's son Elliott—was just twelve. A skier, Elliott wanted to be one of Tabor's aerial all-stars, as Juliet had been.

Bonnie went back to her office. Tabor went back to the little lab he'd used when I was doing my community service. Then, he reappeared.

"What are you up to, Allie?" Tabor said. "I think you may have something that isn't yours. Wouldn't it be wise to give it to me?"

"I don't know what you're talking about."

"I think you do," he said. "Maybe your memory is foggy from the night you went diving and Rob had his little incident. You think anything's seriously wrong with Rob? You think he's maybe about to check out? He doesn't look well."

"Shut up," I said.

"Maybe Bonnie's son will give you some of that comfort you need if Rob doesn't last too long."

"Shut your fat mouth, creep, or I'll call Bonnie."

He turned for the door. "You go ahead and play your

little game. Merry Christmas. My family and I are headed up to Canada to ski for the holidays. It could be a long while before we see each other. Will you miss me?"

I didn't answer but retrieved my files and began doing the filing that was part of my job.

"You shouldn't keep things that aren't yours," Tabor said, from the hall, as he picked up his heavy pea coat. "They could turn out to be bad-luck charms, don't you think?"

I stared down at my files, focusing my eyes so determinedly that my vision swam and the letters on the death certificates blended and danced.

"Allie, do you understand? That could be a bad-luck charm for not just you. For all kinds of people."

"Leave me alone," I said. "Don't mess with me."

"Oh, nobody should mess with you," Tabor said. I felt him step closer, and, unable to help myself, I glanced up. He had his coat over his arm, and he lowered the neck of his collared shirt to reveal miniature riverbeds of raised red flesh. I lowered my eyes again to my big stack of manila folders. I felt rather than heard Tabor move away. When he wanted to be, he was catlike, materializing and dematerializing as though he were not human.

He was not, in fact, human.

A slice of cold air whirled around me as the door opened. "You never got it, Allie," Tabor said softly. "I love her, too."

The door closed. He was gone. If he were smart, he'd never come back.

If he did, though, I would be waiting. I was closer—closer than I'd ever been.

Rob had left me because I couldn't love him until I figured out what had really happened to Juliet, and to these other girls. My loss, and their loss, had to count for something.

A plan began to form at the back of my mind. I would do more than set up the camera Rob had given me as a parting gift. I would do more than monitor Tabor's comings and goings. He wasn't even going to be around. I could take advantage of that time to photograph something else, something that would prove him to be the beast I knew he was. The camera had a waterproof housing. It could withstand pressure up to nearly two hundred feet down.

But I couldn't carry out my plan until after my family had our Christmas. I had to wait, but I didn't have to waste time.

As soon as I saw the lights on Tabor's big truck sweep an arc over the thick verge of black pine at the edge of the parking lot, I turned back to my computer. This time I looked for missing girls. Missing girls who might have some connection with the pendant. Someone who was Japanese. Someone named Sky. For what felt like hours, I kept paging, paging, paging, looking at hundreds of faces on websites from all over the upper Midwest, every seam and shore of Superior. Then I went beyond, to Nebraska and Colorado, Kentucky. A day's drive. Two days. How few girls actually remained missing after a year, or at most, two, was really quite a small number.

Most of them ran away and then turned up, and usually they were repentant, if kind of worse for wear. Some grew up and then got in touch.

Most of the little kids weren't taken by strangers. The parent who didn't have custody kidnapped them. Usually, the young children were found, unharmed.

In a few appalling cases, the father murdered the children to punish the mother. Always the father. The one case of a mother murdering her children, in order to be free to marry a rich man who had no interest in "the daddy thing" was famous and particularly distressing.

I tried to forget about little kids.

The girls that I'd seen chained under the bluff near Tabor Oaks were not children. But they were somebody's children. Somebody was wondering where they were.

No one missing, from anywhere, who could have had those bones seemed to be linked to the necklace, in a way I could imagine.

Sena. Seva. Sienna. Soya. Zoya. Sklyer Schuyler. Skyla.

No Sora.

No Sky.

Not one of those names on anyone missing anywhere. Not for ages. Back I went.

Back for more than two years. More than five.

Chris Olsen and I had to be wrong about what the pendant meant. Or maybe his first suggestion was right: her hobby was stargazing. Someone had loved this girl enough to care about what she loved. Maybe she wasn't Asian at all. Maybe her father or mother did business in Japan. I began to think of her as a person, someone with friends and hobbies.

"He really does scare you, doesn't he?" Bonnie asked suddenly. I jumped in my chair. My back cramped.

"I'm afraid of him," I said finally.

"Can you tell me why? I know he gives you the creeps."

"I don't want to tell you more."

"Allie, I know you think that Tabor had something to do with Juliet's death."

I swallowed. My throat was dry. "How do you know that?"

"It's not because I eavesdrop. I can't help but hear you talking to Rob, sometimes, and it's always about him. It's always about Tabor."

"I . . ." And quickly, before I could repent, I told Bonnie what I knew for sure—how Tabor had abused Juliet sexually when he was her ski coach, the encounters starting when Juliet was only fourteen.

Bonnie's face was impassive. "That's very disturbing," she said.

"You think?"

"Well, he won't hurt you."

"What's to stop him?"

"When you first came to work here, I told you to watch out for him outside the lab. You still have to do that, but really, out there, Allie, he's hardly an unsub . . . He's hardly an unknown commodity . . ."

"A what?" I was sure she'd used the criminal forensic term for "unknown subject." Bonnie went on. "He's well-known in this community. If he were to come anywhere near you in a way that felt threatening, he would stick out like a sore thumb—"

"You called him an 'unsub,'" I interrupted. "That means 'unknown subject.' As in, of an investigation. It's what I've read in my criminology books. Why would you use a word like that?"

"TV," Bonnie said. "I do have some leisure time." Lightly, she touched my back. "You should go home now."

"I've done nothing but sleep. And Rob and I . . . well, he's gone with his family for Christmas, away to Colorado. And we, well, I think we broke up."

"That won't last," Bonnie said. "Everybody breaks up."

"The way he said it, I think it might. Things haven't been right between us since Juliet died."

"How could they be? Neither of you could possibly feel anything but terrible. It's bound to cause some bumps for you two."

For a moment, I let myself believe that Bonnie might be correct—that what had come between Rob and me was a bump, and that we would both pick ourselves up and realize how impossibly dear we were to each other.

Just then, the computer dinged with the result of one of my searches.

Five years ago, a new graduate from Toronto's International High School set out to meet a friend whose family had moved to Minnesota. They intended to backpack across Canada together, after a visit with the friend's family, who lived in . . . Iron Harbor. The Canadian girl never met her friend at the bus stop, as planned. Her family never heard from her. For a year, posters had circulated all around Canada and in Minnesota. A joyous, outdoorsy girl, she loved to ski, camp, and ride horseback. The eldest of four daughters, she wanted to be a physical therapist. In one of the photos on the poster, she wore a red sweater and her gold pendant was clearly visible. It was a gift from her father, a book editor who spoke Japanese fluently. She never took it off.

Her name was Samantha Kelly Young.

Everyone called her Sky.

I4

BLUE CHRISTMAS

BLUE CHRISTMAS

All I could think about was Sky, floating in her grave.
Her parents and sisters were spending another Christmas without her, just as Tommy and Ginny, and I, were spending our first without Juliet.

It didn't exactly make for holiday cheer.

With her native Boston in every syllable, my Grandma Mack showed up the day before Christmas Eve, took one look at me and said, "You in love?" (I nodded miserably.) "That will do it," she said. "I've been in love a dozen times! Twenty! Each one worse than the last."

"You can say that again," my mother muttered.

Matthew Mack, the grandfather I never knew, died in a sailing accident when my mother and her brothers were children. Despite raising three kids alone, my grandmother had been conducting a cheerful search for a second mate.

She was still looking.

"Are you happy, Allie?" my grandmother said.

"Love doesn't make you happy," I told her.

"I'm glad you're figuring that out young," said my mother, who was still pissed at me.

"Thanks, Mom. You were the one that practically talked me into this. You were the one who wanted me to have the right boy at the right time, remember?"

She couldn't deny it.

"I'm going to lie down," I said.

"No, you are not," Jackie told me. "Brian and Carmel will be here any minute, and you are going to make the turkey stuffing while I finish the desserts. And it better be perfect, because you know how Carmel is." My Uncle Brian's wife, Carmel, was beautiful and talented, a musician who was Irish-from-Ireland, but also was some kind of super born-again person. Their two little girls went to a semi-prison religious school that even Brian (a devout Catholic, at least compared with my mother and her other brother) considered, as he put it, "a little much."

The meal had all the makings of a freewheeling disaster.

"Give her a few unraveled Brillo pads and she could knit a Sub-Zero," my mother says of Carmel. And that's when she's being nice.

My mother is suspicious of people who can't be satisfied with a nice DKNY sweater from Macy's but have to prove something by making their own. She's also suspicious of anyone who doesn't have a job outside the home, and she has been known to use the word "parasitic." Carmel always made a big deal about how being a good wife and the best mom possible to Merit and Maria (I found myself think-ing of Bonnie and Chris and how they'd laugh at the name Merit) was "more important than anything I could do in the world." It was all Jackie could do not to curl her lip. This was one of the areas of life where Jackie and I agreed, and I even admired her for sticking to her devoutly independent ways. My mother was basically fearless.

And so was I. I was fearless in most ways . . . except where Garrett Tabor was concerned.

And cooking.

Of course, I also shared my mother's profound lack of proficiency in the kitchen. It bred fear. At my mother's knee, I'd learned to make two things: ground nut stew with sweet potatoes and ginger, and curry, which my mom, a lifelong vegetarian, served as often as other moms served frozen pizza. At least she wasn't going to force tofurkey on us. We were going to have a free-range turkey ("It chose to give up its life," I told Angela) and pumpkin pie. For the latter, my mother, horrifyingly, had butchered a pumpkin, following instructions on a YouTube video. Clearly she had something she wanted to prove to Aunt Carmel, who had offered to bring the pies, the bread, the sides of broccoli, the desserts, the cranberry flip—everything but the tablecloth.

While my grandmother and I chopped onions and celery for the stuffing (my mother would not touch meat and stuffing a dead animal with something was particularly reprehensible to her), Grandma Mack said, "You know the stuffing can really sink a Christmas Eve dinner."

"Thanks, Grandma," I said, my anxiety now trebled.

For something made of wet stale bread and seasoning, it could apparently get complicated. Usually, it's too dry, and people seem to love that: it reminds them of their own mothers, who also were bad cooks. If it's too wet, it's just a nasty gob of ballast, the size of a soccer ball.

Fortunately, there was a YouTube video for sage-and-onion stuffing, too.

Soon, we'd finished it.

My mother was still crafting her two pumpkin pies. We had a public radio station on playing classic-not-cheesy Christmas carols, but that made our own silence even more harrowing. Just as the pies began to smell lovely and aromatic, my uncle and his family arrived—with Carmel and the little girls wearing those kind of discreet but awful matching Christmas sweaters that probably cost two hundred dollars each.

Uncle Brian and Aunt Carmel mixed a bowl of punch for the adults and one for the children and began unloading presents from their car.

My mother took the pies out of the oven. They looked perfect, until the middle of both pies rose as though some kind of demon was trying to fight its way out of a marshmallow Peep. Then each pie sank, leaving a deep depression, like the cone of a tropical storm.

Angela said, "You, like, killed it."

I stared at Angela, wondering if my mother's wrath would cause some kind of physical event like what had happened to the pies. I was glad that Angela, still relatively little and cute, had said this instead of me. This had nothing at all to do with pie: it was a referendum on who was a better mother.

"I can just fill that with meringue," my mother said.

"Meringue doesn't go on pumpkin pie," I said, very slowly. "And I've heard that meringue is a very, very dangerous thing in this very way, like with sinkage. Whipped cream goes on pumpkin pie."

"I could fill that hole with cinnamon ice cream and freeze the whole thing and then put warm brandy on top," my mother said.

"You could put the whole thing in a blender, too."

"Fine," Jackie said. She picked up the phone and called

Sweet Things, claiming the last two pies in Iron Harbor. She said she had an emergency, and she made it sound as if it was a medical emergency, as if people called senior nurses in on holidays for such things. When she put down the phone, her eyes were overly bright, a sign that Jackie might cry. But then, armed with the pies, Mom went outside. As Brian and my grandmother watched, she sailed first one pie and then the second at the path to the woods. She was surprisingly strong about the upper arms, and the pies whapped through the sky like Frisbees.

"Get your coat, Angela," I said, "We're going to the bakery."

"Can I come?" my grandmother asked.

"Nope. She's your daughter."

Angie and I fled, but not before we heard my mother's comment as she came back into the kitchen.

"At least the raccoons will dine well," Mom said.

It was a great dinner. The next morning, I opened Mom's big present to me. A dive camera.

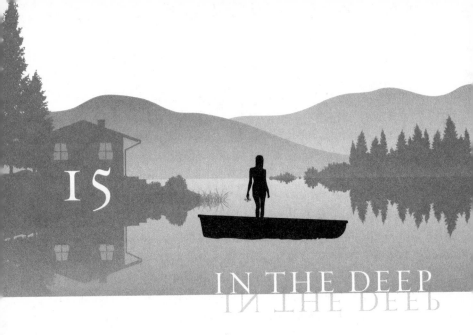

15

IN THE DEEP

IN THE DEEP

It was December 29, a dark day with nothing going on.
My extended family had moved up to The Timbers, the big ski resort on Torch Mountain, where my mother's other brother, Uncle Sean, with his new wife and new baby, would soon join the rest of us. This holiday was a splurge that was always on Grandma Mack's dime: she loved to ski, and we did more night skiing than most families do in two years during those few days. I was a proficient skier, but Angela was a demon, soaring down the Black Diamond runs without benefit of poles. She literally had grown up on skis. Juliet had herself taught Angela, beginning when Angela was only four.

My mother was feeling festive and forgiving and only reminded me to hurry up and join them that night when I said I had some personal and private business to attend to. She assumed it had to do with Skyping Rob and repairing our breach. I only wished that were true.

Since Christmas Eve, although I couldn't blame the stuffing, I had not been feeling my best. Headachy and shaky, I found myself worrying as a second job, making lists of the way my grandmother could get mugged between her house and her car. This, I figured, was the debt from all those sleepless days. This score needed settling. I would expose Garrett Tabor.

For the first time since Rob and I broke up, I would sleep through the day knowing I'd repaid Juliet for her love. I would be able to tell Samantha Kelly Young's family that her daughter had been found—and though their hearts would crack, they would have closure.

The night before, I'd called Wesley, who'd agreed to let me use his little inflatable Odyssey, as well as life jackets and gear. (He was headed out of town with one of the women he annoyingly called "ladies.") I'd lied. I told him that I wasn't planning any diving but wanted to take photos from a few hundred yards out on the lake, when everything was so quiet and still, with eighteen new inches of thick white powder having fallen daintily on Christmas Day. Because there was almost no wind, the cedars and pine were still festooned with frosting, perfect for black-and-white calendar quality shots I needed to complete for a photography class. Since I had keys to Rob's Jeep, I decided to use that, rather than asking my mother to borrow her car.

MOM AND ANGELA dropped me off on their way up to the resort.

"Don't get in any trouble," Mom said. "And don't worry about Rob. That will all heal over once he's home."

"I'm fine," I told her, and, for the first time since our fight, we gave each other a hard hug.

When I arrived, the Tabor Oaks' parking lot was deserted. But I still took the precaution of concealing the Jeep in a little off-road area. I didn't want to risk dropping the keys in the water, so I left the car unlocked, with the keys on the seat. No one would see it. Not one car had passed. With enormous satisfaction, I realized that, looking back, even with my headlamp turned up on high, I could barely make out the outlines of Rob's car. Next to the car, on a tripod, I set up the camera Rob had bought for me, setting it to record five minutes of video every hour for the next four hours.

What had people done before time and date stamps? I could prove when I'd been here and what I'd found, so the links would be unbroken. I had clean copies of the maps Rob and I had made before our first free dive, so when I got out there, I would be able to orient myself easily. The little boat had two solid anchors. What I tried to think about the enormous risk of free diving alone . . . was nothing. As Wesley instructed, there was nothing I could think about that would do me any good. I was putting myself at risk, in a way that was terrifying. Not for the first time, I wished I'd learned to use SCUBA gear.

In the absence of that, I'd taken every safety precaution I could. I'd left my mother a note, letting her know I'd decided to go out on the lake to take pictures, in the impossible event that anything happened to me. I had my phone, fully charged, not that this would do me any good when I was forty feet under icy water. The immensity of the dark lake—no one was around, although the weather was forgiving for December. No one would hear me flail, or scream. No one would notice that dark blue little boat drifting, eventually losing its air, circling like a cork under the white eye of the moon. The big seawater. I could not crowd my head with all that lay beneath.

If I were lucky, I'd be down, get the photos, and be up again within minutes—home again for a hot shower and to tear that note into tiny pieces.

If I got unlucky—that didn't bear thinking about. At least my mother wouldn't be like the Youngs, and never know.

As I left the parking lot and hiked down to the little natural harbor where Wesley said he would leave the beached Odyssey, crazy things ballooned in my mind. It was as though I were asleep and dreaming, despite never having been more alert and awake.

What if the bodies were dummies? They could be faked. Anything could be faked.

The boathouse brides—why did I think of them this way?—in the caves seemed now to me like images from a Disney thrill ride.

I'd seen dead bodies before, but never so old and so macerated by their environment.

They had to be real.

But what if I was doing all this for nothing? What if they were old Halloween decorations?

As I checked out the equipment in the boat and slipped into the layer I would wear under my dry suit, I felt the imprint of my ring and the little pendant, on their chain next to my skin.

That wasn't faked. I had seen that girl's smiling face—her short, carefree curly hair.

I finished suiting up. I checked my long blade fins, my hood and gloves, my weight belt, my camera's flash and housing, and the double clip that attached it to a harness I snapped around my chest.

You can be scared and still be doing the right thing.

With a penlight on a clipboard attached to the maps, I quietly motored out to where Rob and I had gone with Wesley.

Carefully, I slipped both anchors into the water and made

sure the boat was secure and would not drift. In the water-proof case I'd brought for this purpose, I stowed my phone and the clipboard. I breathed gently and centered myself as I secured my weight belt and fitted my mask, twice for safety. *Alexis,* I thought, *a prayer to the grown woman I will one day become, be with me. Rob and Juliet are with me. Protect me, and help me prevail.*

Then I dived.

I had luckily moored even closer to the ruins of the old boathouse in the cliff, because I saw it right away. Closer, I swam. There was the opening to the little man-made "cave," that I now remembered looking like the doorway to some sort of elfin chapel. They were chained right inside the door.

Except they weren't.

The chains were there.

Among the chains, tangled in their coils, there were a few bits of fabric, including what once might have been a shred of Samantha Kelly Young's scarlet sweater. But the girls were gone.

He'd moved them. They had to be in one of these other pocked, small openings. But where? Who knew? Garrett Tabor could have come out here, at his leisure, in his own dry suit with ninety minutes of oxygen. He could have moved them one at a time. He could have brought a boat, a little inflatable or a big boat, and taken the brides up, wrapped them in sailcloth, just the way I'd seen him do with someone or something long ago. Perhaps he put them in his truck and buried them on a lonely hillside, deep among the thick trees? It wouldn't have been difficult; they would not have been heavy. There was nothing left but rags.

Zeroing in on the piece of what looked like knitted cloth, I snapped ten pictures. I could not find even a strand of bright blonde hair or a shred of bone. How could he have so thoroughly eliminated every trace of them? He was the medical examiner's son, that's how. He was a trained nurse. He knew how to clean up.

Could I have found the wrong part of the boathouse? I was sure I wasn't wrong. It looked exactly the same as what I remembered from that night—but of course, that night had exploded in the terror of Rob's faint and Tabor's "rescue."

I snapped more pictures.

Well, I had done it once. I was not uncomfortable, or panicky, only enraged.

I could do it again. If I had to, I'd learn how to use oxygen tanks and I'd search.

At that moment, a big shadow passed overhead. At first I thought, oh hell, that's the legendary ten-foot-long sturgeon. But the shadow wasn't fast moving. It was broad and flat. No! It had to be the little boat. The boat was drifting. I had to get up there, and fast, or I'd find myself stranded three hundred yards from shore and lose Wesley's boat on top of it.

With prudent speed (I couldn't risk the bends), stopping every three feet for a couple of seconds to clear my ears, I made my way through the darkness toward that shadow. When I broke the surface, I put my hands out for the ladder. There it was—but the boat was bigger, more solid than the little Odyssey.

A strong hand grabbed my dive hood, ripping it from my head.

"Little Allie," said Garrett Tabor. "Happy New Year."

On instinct, I kicked away from his boat: small and sleek with a little outboard motor. He easily kept up with me, smiling, casually swiping at me with one of the oars, aiming for the back of my head and hitting me hard on the shoulder.

I shrieked into my mask, and then shook it off. I kept stroking.

He could have killed me right then, pulled a gaff hook from the bottom of that boat and put it through my head and watched me spiral down with a ribbon of my blood trailing. Instead, he stood up and drew the oar up over his head. He would like it, I thought, if it looked as though I'd hit my head and drowned.

The beach was directly to my left. The rocks were in front of me.

I reached up, flipped my headlamp off, and dived.

The one thing Garrett Tabor didn't count on, as he tried to follow me, was that I could hold my breath for a very long time.

Shedding my fear like a layer of ice, I clasped my hands over my camera and scissored toward the rocks that made the natural shoulders of the little beach where Wesley had wound one of the lines from the Odyssey around a round boulder. When my gloved hands touched rock, I began to climb, scrabbling for traction on the slippery dark teeth of the cliffs. I kicked off my blade fins and let them fall. In the dive booties that protected me from the worst cuts, I staggered to my feet.

Tabor was still a hundred yards out. I could see him making a slow circle in the boat. He couldn't even see me, my black suit against the dark rocks. Silently as only a Parkour tracer could, I made my way over the uneven surface of the tumbled rocks. Then I came to a crevasse. I could jump it. But this close in, there could be ice on those rocks. If I fell and went down between them, breaking my leg or knocking myself out, he wouldn't have to kill me. I'd have done it on my own.

I decided to take the risk. For an instant, to "derive" the course ahead, I switched on my lamp. Immediately, I heard Garrett Tabor's shout of rage and heard the motor spring to life. But I did not think of him: this was *parcours du combattant*, like an obstacle course used to train soldiers—except it was war, for real. The distance was perhaps six feet. My *Saut de Précision* (precision jump) would have to be perfect and, for the first time, completely blind.

Mom, Rob, Juliet, I thought, and I leaped.

David Belle would have been elated. I hit the opposite rock, dropped and rolled off. Then I beat it up the beach across the parking lot, my miner's light full on as I made Rob's Jeep, nimbly located the keys, and roared out of the protective cover of the fir trees.

TWO HOURS LATER, washed clean, my hair curled, and a menthol patch on my throbbing shoulder, (an Aurora Borealis of bruises by morning), I was in our family's chalet on Torch Mountain, sipping a glass of champagne and feeling about as powerful as I'd ever felt in my entire life.

He hadn't gone to Canada. He'd followed me. He'd lain in wait for me.

But I'd beaten him. I'd beaten him!

And yet, he knew exactly what I was going to do. I put my glass down.

Garrett Tabor derived *me*. He'd seen where he needed to go to get me, like a Parkour trace.

Bonnie was wrong.

I would never be safe, even in a crowd, as long as he was alive.

I decided to find out more about the boss I never saw. Although I'd known the Tabors as the face of the Tabor Clinics all my life, I didn't really know them at all. I was a kid, and how much did you really know about people who looked after your health but were not your friends or family?

Later that night, I asked my mother how Dr. Stephen's wife had died.

"It was way before my time here," my mother said. We were taking down the tree, packing each of the ornaments away in a tall box of drawers, each nested with cardboard cups. "But I know it was a car wreck. I know that it was terrible."

AT WORK, I began looking for old obituaries on newspaper databases.

There was a front-page item in the *Minneapolis Star-Tribune*, dated more than twenty years earlier. The headline read TABOR CLINIC FOUNDER FAMILY DEAD IN CHRISTMAS CRASH.

Inside, I turned to the obituary for the child who would have been Garrett Tabor's youngest sister.

Rachel Whitcomb Green Tabor, born December 24, died exactly three years later, on December 24. She was the daughter and third-born child of Merry Whitcomb Green and Stephen Tabor. The other children were Garrett, Gavin, and Rebecca.

Merry Whitcomb Green (the name made me sad) also died in the accident—in which an eighteen-wheeler hit black ice and crushed the passenger side of the family's station wagon. She would have celebrated her thirtieth birthday the next day. She was born on Christmas.

The mother's and the little girl's birthdays were just one day apart. Both at Christmastime.

No wonder the poor man didn't date.

Briefly, I scanned newspaper articles about a subsequent lawsuit against the company that owned the truck, a drunk driver, and a colossal settlement. Unwillingly, I felt awful for Dr. Stephen's family.

The youngest of the children, Gavin Tabor, was physically disabled. He was a baby, not even one year old. The accounts of the trial reported that he would need years of physical rehabilitation. He would be twenty-something now, and . . . that was where I was forced to give up the thread.

Bonnie called me and asked if I'd finished my filing.

"I was daydreaming," I told Bonnie.

"Well, there's nothing wrong with daydreaming. But I have a job for you. A real job. I just want you to do it. It will be a challenge for you."

I almost laughed. "What if I mess it up?"

"I don't know anything about the forensic side of it, but I do know that he has more of the materials that you'd be working on. Dr. Steve did say to tell you that your work would be part of the permanent file, however."

Again, random niceness. What gives? I thought.

What Dr. Stephen had left was an actual piece of evidence from a "situation," with instructions on how to examine it for possible use. There was no further information. Nothing that told me where the evidence had come from or what kind of death scene, or crime scene, was involved.

Dr. Stephen wrote that I should use ordinary care in following the steps and go as far as I could without the need for another tier of chemical analysis. He left me a paper cloth lab cap to prevent my hair from contaminating the evidence, and several pairs of disposable gloves, pointing out in his note that most people cut theirs up accidentally, because they were trying so hard not to. I was to use the instruments I thought would be most useful.

The evidence was a torn piece of blue fabric.

With surgical scissors, I cut off a small square and, from comparing it with other samples, determined that it was the kind of denim used in less expensive blue jeans. It was blood-stained and dirty, as though it had been pulled from the ground. Using tweezers, I placed the cloth on a light table. For an hour, I picked off particles.

I found three different kinds of plant matter—broken needles I identified as coming from a black pine, tufts of fescue, both green and brownish, and some kind of ground cover. I also found sand, soil, and two kinds of hair, one coarse and dark reddish-brown, one shorter and very pale.

Laying the cloth on a light box, I immediately saw a series of small rips, irregular, but each similar to the one next to it.

I photographed everything with one of the lab's Polaroids.

Then, my hands sweating, I scraped a bit of the dark matter staining the cloth into a glass dish and added a bit of Luminol.

It wasn't blood.

Leaning close, I followed human instinct and sniffed. The smell was familiar, and recently familiar.

What could have the consistency of blood and smell so sweet?

It was syrup! It was some kind of syrup, from something like the blueberry ice cream that Angela and I had made a few weeks back.

But, could I assume it was all blueberry syrup? Hesitantly, I scraped another particle from the other side of the ripped cloth. This immediately reacted. Blood. I didn't know if it was human blood, but it was blood.

The small light pieces of hair appeared to be human.

The thick brownish tufts were not. They were hair from an animal.

I glanced up at the clock and saw that it was after 2 A.M. My shoulder was barking with pain. But this was too interesting to quit, even though my shift was over. I gulped down Advil. After I'd catalogued my findings and separately bagged and labeled them, I filled out the sheets Dr. Stephen had left. Then I wrote him a note, thanking him for the gift and his complimentary words, which I left in his inbox with the forms from John Jay that would give me my internship credit. I also filled out my time card.

Bonnie and I got ready to leave.

"So are you going to tell me?"

"Sure," she said. "What did you figure out?"

I explained my findings, and as our cars warmed up, Bonnie and I shared a cup of tea in the little break room. She told me what I had been studying.

"That was a case of a little child mauled by a bear," she said. "It was up near the Boundary Waters, just last week, a family having Christmas at their year-round vacation cabin."

"Was the child killed?" I asked. I didn't understand why people were stupid enough to take really little kids, who would think grizzly bears were cute and cuddly, up into the wilderness. The Boundary Waters is fifteen hundred square miles of pristine lakes and camping areas, part of it in Canada and part of it in Minnesota. The cabin must have been just outside the park area because no one lived there year-round, or at all, except the rangers.

Bonnie shook her head. "No, but the child's grandfather died."

She went on to say that the decision was made not to

find and kill the bear, because, well, the bear wasn't hunting. It didn't eat the person's body. The man had left scraps of a pancake breakfast out to lure the animal so the child could see it. They had a big truck, but it wouldn't start. The grandmother was afraid to move her husband, because he was so badly hurt, so she drove the child to the hospital in a little VW Beetle they kept up there. "By the time the ambulance got there, he had bled out," Bonnie said. "People make animals look like geniuses."

It was then that I learned about Bonnie's husband, who died young from complications of flu. He had been a newspaper reporter, a fly fisherman who had loved the Boundary Waters. The chance to go camping up there with her sons, to help them remember their dad, which she would do again at spring break, had been part of the reason she'd moved up here. She smiled and gave me a hug as we parted.

"The other reason was you," she said.

"You didn't even know I existed," I said. She was such a good person.

"I knew I'd meet you," she said.

Breathless, I asked about Dr. Stephen's family tragedy.

"I don't know everything, but I know he never got over it. He has some photos in there. He and his wife apparently competed as dancers, like jive dancers. Can you imagine that? I don't think he ever got over her, or the little girl." Bonnie paused. "I read that obituary, too, when I came here. And it was weird."

"How?"

"I looked up the inquest, I'm afraid. I was curious."

"Why?" I pushed Bonnie for more. She was reluctant, I could tell.

"Well, the little girl didn't die in the crash. I guess Stephen could tell his wife was dead, and he went in the ambulance with his baby. I gather she was bleeding from a head wound. It was no more than five minutes. The little girl was restrained in her car seat on the driver's side and she was crying, and apparently, Stephen testified that he gave her a superficial once-over and she seemed unharmed. He could hear the other ambulance and the fire trucks coming, so he left her there with Garrett, who would have been, what? Fifteen? Sixteen?"

My very blood slowed down. "What happened?"

"She stopped breathing. A kid that little, in the cold? They should have been able to save her. It was a long time ago, but still . . ."

"How do they know she just stopped breathing?"

"That was what Garrett Tabor told them," Bonnie said.

That little girl was his sister.

SOME WOMEN

SOME WOMEN

For a week after Juliet disappeared—and again, after her body was found in the river—I had sessions on the phone with a counselor, a psychologist. The next morning, I woke up from what psychologist described as an ordinary anxiety dream: someone I couldn't see was chasing me, and my legs were so tired that I couldn't go on. I kept glancing back over my shoulder and begging my feet to move, as the fog behind me resolved itself into a solid shape, a human form. I couldn't take another step. Lightning stabbed the ground around me: lightning with form, a man's shape.

How is this ordinary?

My right shoulder blade felt three times the size of my left. I could barely raise my arm to the level of my chest. If I hadn't had the good sense (and the good mantras-for-life from Jackie) I'd probably have it in a sling by now.

I wanted to call the police.

Garrett Tabor had hurt me, and he'd hurt me badly. When-ever I thought of just going ahead and calling, of explaining everything, I thought of those photos of my family blooming on my phone, one after another.

What could I tell the police about what Tabor had done to me, without risking some kind of retribution from him? How could I prove he'd smacked my shoulder black and blue with an oar? I already knew the answers. I wouldn't be able to prove it. My mother would find out I'd been diving, alone, and that I put myself at his mercy. Down would come the hammer. It was suspended over me by the slenderest of threads since the consequences of our first (and last) free dive.

I sat up and decided, no matter what, I would call.

Then I remembered that my phone was still in that boat, and, as such, was probably now a cube of frozen circuits. Of course, Jackie was a nurse manager for a hospital emergency room. We had a landline. We had two.

I stared at the house phone, and imagined telling Tommy Sirocco, Juliet's dad, about Garrett Tabor chasing me in his boat . . . injuring me with an oar. I pictured telling him that this happened after I dived to discover he moved skeletonized bodies he'd chained to ruins of a boathouse in a cliff thirty feet under the surface of the lake.

Bodies that were no longer there.

Bodies I couldn't prove had ever been there.

Tommy was protective of me. Tommy would believe me.

But if I were a detective assigned to this case, I would wonder why there was so much bun and no burger. I had bruises, but I'd been climbing on icy rocks. The Odyssey was out there . . . I still had to figure out how to recover Wesley's Odyssey—which didn't even *belong* to him but to the dive shop where he worked—and which had probably drifted to Michigan by now. Put this all together and it spelled nothing.

Peeking out of my door to make sure the shades in the

living room and kitchen were all pulled tight, I nipped into the bathroom.

When I came out, I noticed my mom. My mother was awake, sitting at the kitchen table, gazing into space. Strange. She would have been home for a long time, since midnight. "Did you pull a double?" I asked. She was about to earn her PhD, and it had been years since she worked a double shift. She only switched to PMs, from three to eleven, after Juliet died, to be with me more often. Although it could get her spinning biorhythmically, the change had worked in Jackie's favor: she worked two weeks straight, including weekends at the ER, and then had ten full days off. And as it turned out, she loved it. But I had no idea what she was doing at the kitchen table at nine in the morning. If I hadn't awakened unexpectedly, I would never have seen her. So when I came out, I sat down with her. She didn't seem to see me.

"Did you hear me, Mom?"

Jackie looked at me then, but not as though she really saw me.

"What are you doing up?" she said.

"Well, I had a nightmare. But I could ask you the same."

Angela was at school. From my sleep world, which was never fully curtained off from the Daytimers' world: I heard the flow of their comings and goings, the deliveries of mail and packages, the exodus from the bus at 3 P.M., the traffic at 4 P.M. My mother would have been there when Angela left for school. She always was. I was there after school. Always. I slapped down a bee of panic. Tabor was not going to grab my little sister.

Taking down our jar of cinnamon sticks and the sugar bowl, and my herbal sleepy tea, I began to boil water. Questioning, I held out two cups.

"Mmmmm. Thanks. I need some," said my mother. "I did work a double. We had a bad car accident last night. Mother and two little girls. The smaller girl is just hanging on. The older sister is fine. Mom is dead. I sort of wanted to stand in with the little one until the grandmother came, all the way back from Saint Petersburg. And then, you can imagine, the grandmother went wild. She saw them yesterday morning."

"Awww, no," I said. "That's terrible. From around here?"

"Nope. The grandmother is. The mom and the children, from Chicago. On the way home. Car filled with Barbies. Shit." She picked up her computer bag and headed for the stairs. Then she came back and kissed my head. "I forgot my tea."

"You don't have to stay up."

"Did you hear from Rob?"

"Just a postcard. He won't be back until . . . until the end of the week. And I don't know, you know?"

"He's being stubborn."

"It's more than that, Mom," I said. "I know Rob loves me, but something is wrong and it's more than that he wants us to go on with our lives after Juliet." As I said this, I realized that I had known, for a long time, that this was really true. Rob didn't keep anything from me. He never had.

"You'll figure it out," Jackie said. "Keep communicating. Don't put up walls."

"I'm not the one who's putting up walls, Jack-Jack," I said. "This is all his choice. I'm sure he's getting with the ski bunnies in Vail." A beautiful picture of my beautiful guy entwined in the dark with some girl with a movie-star ass quickly turned my stomach sour.

"Well, write me up as a victim of disappointment in Rob's character then. I'm beat, and I guess I can talk to you tonight.

I guess I can. It will keep until tonight. I'm just . . . dazed. I just didn't let myself feel it." She made for the spiral staircase that led up to her room, but dragging, and I was alarmed until she added, "Don't call me Jack-Jack."

Whatever it was didn't sound like it would keep until tonight, but I wasn't about to cause her to fret even more.

I could hear her moving about up there, doing her own bed-time prep. The whole second floor was my mother's bedroom, library, and study. Up there, she had her own refrigerator. She and Gina took Mondays off from their run, so Mom would probably sleep until afternoon. She loved sleep. As someone who never got enough, she considered sleep near-sexual in pleasure. Her king-sized Australian basswood bed, with nine pillows, belonged in a castle. She reasoned that, as a single mother of forty with two young daughters, she was never going to need the kind of privacy a woman of thirty-three with no young daughters might need. When she met Mr. Right, she told Gina, (cliché although it was) it would be in the emergency room, where he'd just suffered his serious bout of chest pains over a slight decline in his six million shares of Disney stock. The wedding would be in Monaco.

I drank both cups of tea. I was starving, but if I ate what I wanted, which was Brie with pickles and pimentos on whole wheat, I might never sleep. I settled for a handful of shortbread, left over from my Aunt Carmel's largesse. Carmel was perhaps the best cook I had ever known, better even than Mrs. Dorn, who made her own bread every day. After the epic pie-throwing incident, these words would never cross my lips.

I could see how women ended up tipping the scales at two hundred pounds as a result of depression. Men were iffy. Brie never let you down.

Where was Rob tonight?

How was he rounding out the last days at Heavenly? Tears pooled in the corners of my eyes, stinging. How dare he dump me for trying to do good? How dare he dump me at all? I didn't even care that he'd dumped me. All I wanted was to hold him and kiss him and smell his hair and the hollow of his neck. All I wanted was for him to love me still.

I sat back to read a book of essays debunking traditional religions.

Dr. Andrew, my mother's boss, was a devout Lutheran, two words that didn't seem to link up. As I see it, Lutherans are a sort of default religion, like vanilla, neither as frankly and joyously wacked as Pentecostals nor so joylessly and grimly superior as Catholics. Dr. Andrew had given the book to my mother to read, because it troubled him. He considered his faith his compass, he told my mom.

In some religions, people don't believe in life after death (and I guess that if I had a religion, it would be one of those kinds; I think that one life is more than enough). For those people, immortality is human memory.

If that were true, Juliet certainly was alive, still.

A zombie angel.

How I loved her.

Her parents and grandparents and her cousins loved her as much as Rob and I did. Even little ski fans, who'd never met Juliet Sirocco but had seen film of her flying like a whirling blade through the sky above the slopes, taking every chance and no prisoners, they loved her, too.

And Garrett Tabor . . .

I sat up on the leather recliner, my book tumbling to the floor.

That last night at the lab, Tabor, referring to Juliet, had said, *I love her, too.*

I love her.

Not in the past tense.

Garrett Tabor was too smart to make mistakes with ordinary speech. Every moment he was near me, he was playing me. He knew exactly what he was saying.

What did he mean? That Juliet was still alive somewhere? Or that his love for her was still alive?

The thought exhausted me. I put my head back on the leather cushion of the chair and started to drift off, when suddenly, I was aware of another person in the room. Jerking to an instant salute, I sat up and saw my mother, who had pulled up a chair and was sitting across from me.

"I didn't come home late just because of the accident," she said. "There was another reason."

She looked funny. She looked more worn out than usual, and she usually looked more worn out than she should have. For a moment, the funny way she looked made me afraid. I thought for sure she was going to tell me that she'd had a bad mammogram, although she wasn't even old enough to have regular mammograms.

I said, "Mom, what's wrong?"

"Nothing," she said. "Really nothing. I just have to talk to you."

She didn't look like it was "nothing, really nothing."

My mother said, "There are going to be clinical trials, starting in March. I wanted to be the one to tell you this. A Danish geneticist, of all things, has teamed up with Andrew and they have permission for clinical trials for . . . well . . . for . . ."

"Me."

As a person who worked full-time, who had a relatively young child, and a daughter with a condition, Jackie was pushing herself way too hard to finish her PhD, a degree that had taken people as long as five years. (Have I mentioned that this was all voluntary? I had not seen my father outside a Skype screen since I was in preschool, but he'd recently been promoted to chair of his department at Seattle Mercy, and was also a full professor. Not only that, he now had normal IVF twin boys—so his guilt checks were ever more handsome and did not look to be decreasing, even with my increasing age.) Naturally, my mother's dissertation was on a specific genetically transmitted chronic condition, and naturally, her dissertation dealt with a very specific kind of gene therapy that would convince the DNA of the XP person to copy itself as normal.

She had finished her dissertation over the summer.

This was all still theoretical. Until now.

"Wow," I said.

"Yes."

"I'm glad you finished your dissertation," I said. "Before it became outmoded."

"Me, too," she said. "But that's . . ."

I finished for her: "That's biology for you!" My mother says this about pretty much everything except the weather. I asked, "What are the horrible mutagenic side effects? What will grow out of my forehead?"

"There aren't any that they see. The first trial is in March and the next one is in October. Here. Not Denmark."

That sucks. I wanted to go to Denmark.

Then I said, "Nausea, vomiting, headaches, irritability, joint pain, constipation, dizziness or vision problems that, in rare cases, could be the sign of a potentially life-threatening condition?"

"No, wise guy," my mother said, and two perfect movie tears formed in each of her eyes. "You're already part of the longitudinal study, and have been for more than ten years, so you'll automatically be part of the first group. I can't decide about waiting for the second group or going ahead. That's up to you, I suppose."

"Holy cow."

"Yes, Allie. Holy cow indeed."

"How did you handle finding out?"

"It was a rumor that was running around for a while, but we all figured, years from now. Everything is always years from now. Then, yesterday, Andrew told us the game was on. He didn't want to tell any of us until all the approvals were secured. The Danish scientist is an MD. I spoke to your dad last night . . . yes! I spoke to your dad about him. Louis knew all about him."

I didn't know what to say in response. I scoured my memory for the last time I'd heard my mother refer to my father by his given name, Louis, and that page of my memory was unmarked by a single recollection.

She went on. "This guy found out something by accident, last summer, that made it all fit. The best things happen as the result of mistakes, sometimes. Like, the obvious example is penicillin. That went from nothing to the standard in a few years."

"Why is the obvious example penicillin?"

"You know why. It was bread mold."

"That's not my discipline, Jack-Jack."

My mother got up and slid into the big chair next to me. "This could be the key," she said. "It makes sense, that's why I'm hopeful. It could be your chance to be . . . like anyone else. I mean, better. But do anyone-else things. Like . . . go diving in a place that isn't cold and dark."

She meant me, of course, but she meant herself, too. Not diving. Being like anyone else's mother. You couldn't blame her.

Unreasonably, I thought of Rob's father.

Mr. Dorn ("Just call me Dennis, just Dennis") didn't ski, although Rob's mother, who had been a champion tennis player in college, was not only an avid skier but also an amateur athlete of every kind. Mr. Dorn sold sporting goods equipment, but a little jogging and the occasional five hundred rounds of golf with clients were about it for him. Still, he sat in the cold until midnight, at the bottom of the runs, to watch Rob hiss down to a flourishing stop. He even came up to Torch when we skied. He did it all the time.

Sometimes, I thought, this is what Mr. Dorn gets with Rob—the glorious now. This is what he gets in place of a future. This could be his whole life as a father. And it seemed that the Dorns were more or less at peace with that. .

My mother, ferociously, was not. She never had been. She would force me to be well by sheer force of will.

When I was little, my mom took me to a support group with other XP children, several of them older and already sicker than I. The counselor led us to draw things we wanted to do and be, and without exception, everyone drew something impossible. They wanted to be tennis players, not design ping-pong tables. They wanted to be rock singers, not studio musicians. What kid wouldn't?

Of course, the counselor led us around to see how we could be what we wanted, sort of—which meant human-not-really. My mother got pissed off. This is not that uncommon for her. After three meetings, she began to sigh really loudly.

After four meetings, she said, "Could you frame this more hopelessly if you tried? You're telling them to be happy with less. Kids aren't *supposed* to be happy with less. It's not . . . biological. Kids aren't supposed to want less. They're supposed to want everything."

"Mrs., uh, Flynn," the psychologist said, doing what people always did, looking at my mother and assuming that "Kim" was a misprint. "I have a PhD in counseling and guidance . . ."

"And I have an RN," snapped Jackie, who didn't yet have her master's at the time. "Even I know that you don't tell kids to start giving up their dreams as job one." She stared at the counselor's feet. "Like you. You wanted to be a ballerina. And you went pretty far with that before you got too . . . too busty. But you could have made costumes for other girls who weren't as good as you were, when you were little. You could have helped them to be Giselle, when you wanted to be Giselle yourself. Why didn't you do that?"

The message suggesting that we might be happier outside "group" was waiting on the answering machine when we got home. My mother would sooner have taken me to a class in ritual sacrifice. I asked her, how did you know the lady wanted to be a ballerina?

Of course, Jackie said, it was both nature and nurture: the slight ducky-ness of a dancer's stance, taught young, lasts forever.

"Are you happy?" my mother said to me that night, finally.

"I'm happy," I said. "I don't want to be too happy."

"I know," my mom said. "The thing about happy is you can't protect yourself from being too devastated by not anticipating the best. It turns out that you might as well hope for the best because it doesn't change the outcome."

"In movies, guys say they'll never love anyone again, except the girl who died, because they could never bear to feel that kind of loss."

"That," my mother said, "is a cheap way for men in movies to get sex without commitment. Not that this is that bad an idea, in some very specific circumstances."

Too much information. The last time I'd visited her at the ER, my mom had been leaning back against a counter in an undeniably sexy pose, smiling up at some college-aged guy she introduced to me as "Trent." It just got worse; the doctors looked like they should be dating me. Pretty soon, they would look like my younger brothers. I blotted out the image of my mother having sex with someone who didn't need to shave every day. The blotting was difficult because I did suspect from a few things Gina had said that my mother was thinking about dating someone. I didn't know who the lucky suitor was, and Jackie was not confiding—in me, at least. But I felt sure that he was younger.

On the other hand, every square inch of my skin was about to combust with longing for Rob's touch, and my mother had been single for thirteen years. Who was I to judge her? I knew that she would gratefully be celibate for the rest of her life if I could be well.

We both sat quietly in the chair for minutes. Then I said, "It's too late for Juliet."

Jackie said, "It is."

My throat caught. "Just such a little bit too late," I said.

She nodded. "Everything about this is wonderful except that part. It was not the first thing I thought, but it was up there. I will have to tell Ginny and Tommy myself. I don't

want them to hear it on some news report about the clinic." I
wanted to go on talking, but Jackie got up and hugged me so
hard she knocked the breath out of me.

"I won't sleep, though. It's like Christmas morning."

I was almost as happy for her as I was for myself.

Happier.

18

THE PAST DARK

THE PAST DARK

That day, which turned out to be the last day of even-close-to-normal, I didn't end up sleeping very much, either.

Finally, sensing it was dark, I decided to hell with pride and everything else. I would call Rob. I couldn't wait to talk to Rob.

Everything was changed.

We'd had a fight, or at least, he'd had a fight . . . or something, but the news about the clinical trials trumped that. It couldn't even wait three more days until he got home. I thought I remembered him mentioning that his uncle was bringing his kids out there, too, after Christmas, so I knew Rob would be busy. The news about clinical trials was too good to keep to myself.

How would it be to go on our honeymoon in St. Lucia? How would it be to go hiking in a sunny mountain meadow? We might actually be able to . . . do things. We might have experiences so lush and light-filled that I could hardly ever think of them real. You had to pay to get to them, but the experiencing, the memories, anything your senses could accommodate—that was all free. How could anyone ever be bored in a world where there was sun?

For me, the thought of the possibility of being able to do things the way Daytimers did was like being blind and trying to imagine the color orange. I certainly knew what it felt like to be out in the sun, under my protective gear, but to feel its heat? Unafraid?

I took our phone into my room, and I called him.

No answer.

Ducking downstairs, I liberated my mother's phone from her purse and sent texts asking Rob if he'd heard the news from his parents, hoping that referring to "the news" would pique his curiosity. Then, I carried Jackie's cell phone around like I was in seventh grade in case a text pinged. Nothing. Finally, I looked up the resort called Heavenly, called the desk, and asked if I could speak to anyone in the Dorn family. The phone rang and rang. Finally, the operator at the hotel took a message.

Roiling, I left a note for my mom and took Angie directly from the bus to the movies. Mom was nowhere in evidence, although the car was there. This normally would have spiked fear in me, at least since the cavalcade of Tabor's surveillance photos of my family; but now, I thought she might be at a meeting about the clinical trials or having an afternoon delight with a resident named Spencer.

At 4 P.M., it was already more or less dark. There was a new cartoon horror flick at the mall halfway between Iron Harbor and Duluth, based on a crazy Neil Gaiman story about twin babies raised by doting vampire godparents. So we hunched in our seats and ate our way through that—consuming two tubs of popcorn with double butter and brewer's yeast. Afterward, we drove back home to Gitchee for a real meal. At 6:30 P.M., the town was as dark as midnight.

The place was deserted.

Gid sat in a booth by himself, reading the Sunday *New York Times*. His new wife (I'd never spoken more than three words to her) was spinning around on one of the stools at the bar. On this early January night, an older couple sharing a modest foccacia were his only guests.

Angela and I sat down in the booth.

"You hungry?" Gid said.

"Always," Angela answered.

Out of deference to our mom, we ordered vegetarian: a large double-cheese with mushrooms, onions, olives, pineapple, sun-dried tomatoes, roasted eggplant, and two kinds of bell peppers. We insisted on paying, although I hadn't paid Gid for food since middle school. To defeat me, he gave us two pizzas and a jug of homemade cream soda.

While we ate, he sat with us.

"I get depressed after Christmas," he said. "I get depressed before, too."

"I think that's common," I offered.

"I'm very depressed," Angela said. "My cousins, Merit and Mia, have a budget for clothes for a year, and it's five hundred dollars. Each. They're like . . . eight years old." Angela wouldn't be ten until May, so this made both Gid and I laugh.

"Go play pinball," I told Angie, giving her seven quarters.

As soon as she was happily bashing away at the machine, Gid said, "Where's Rob?"

"Colorado. He went skiing in Vail with his parents. I think some cousins came out there, too. His dad's sisters and their kids."

"Bet that's beautiful."

"You've never been?"

"Never been out West. Never farther away than Tennessee. And wherever the team went. Florida once. And then only two years." Gideon looked at me as though I'd asked a question, which I hadn't. "Yes, Allie. I went to college. Baseball scholarship. A full ride."

"What position did you play?"

"Pitcher. Like Cy Young. He was a Lac du Flambeau Chippewa. An Indian like me. You've heard of the Cy Young award." I hadn't, and I didn't care, but something in Gid's eyes made me nod.

"Why only two years? What happened?"

"I wrecked my arm. Rotator cuff. It's common for young guys. I spent a year rehabbing it. I got back in and wrecked it again. The doctor said if I didn't stop I could lose the use of the arm. So I came home. Got married. My father was a cook up at the Timbers. We bought this place together. We bought up land, wherever we could. Rentals. Cabins. Real estate. My dad retired to Tennessee. Him and my mom have a cabin on Stirrup Lake that's the size of a strip mall. Three stories. He did good. Me, too. I don't have to do this, Allie." I realized then that I had no idea how old Gideon was. He could have been forty or sixty. "I like running this place because I get aggravated if I'm not around people. Plus, I don't want the Tabors to buy it no matter what the price. But I could live on what I have forever, and leave plenty to my sons."

"That's great, though, Gid. You didn't have one dream. But you got another." So far as I knew, however, he didn't yet have any sons, although he'd recently married again.

"I would give it all up to have played two seasons in the show."

"What show?"

"Pro ball."

"Well," I said. "I'm sorry. What did you want to study?"

"Playing ball. College was nothing to me without it. That was all I wanted to do. You going to college, Allie?" Just him saying that lit an electric wire in my chest. All I'd thought about was Rob, and my last encounter with the mad Mr. Tabor, and then the clinical trials. But next week, I would be a freshman in college. Life just kept contriving and contriving, the way Thornton Wilder said.

"In ten days, Gid."

"You graduated?"

"Early."

"What do you want to do? Where are you going?"

"I'm not going anyplace but my room. It's all online, because of my . . . you know." Angie came back. This time Gideon dug deep into the pockets of his work pants and pulled out a fistful of quarters for her. "I'm going to study criminal justice. I want to be a forensic scientist."

"This because of Juliet?"

"It was true before Juliet. But sure, more now."

"Why before?"

"Gid, that time when Garrett Tabor chased me over here?"

Without warning, Gideon stood, pulled a rag out off a shelf nearby and began swabbing the table. His jaw flickered. He retrieved a white box with a laughing chef on it and began to pack up the quarter of the pizza Angie and I had left, packing another box with the one we hadn't touched. Then he said under his breath, "That piece of shit."

"I know he's bad, Gideon. He's really bad. He's done bad things, and I can't prove it even though I've seen the proof."

"How bad?"

The room suddenly felt very small and hot, and my voice very loud. My head began to pound as though the veins were bursting; the pizza threatened to boil up at the back of my throat. "As bad as you can do, Gideon."

"Like he killed somebody."

"Like that. Yes."

He nodded without so much as a blink. "I have known that bastard all his life and all of mine. Even when he was a kid, he gave me the creeps. He would pick girls up at the bus stop, girls who came up here from Chicago? Or down from Canada? Bring them in here. I would hear him talking about his family's chalets and their ski stores and how they owned this whole town. And the girls would just be dazzled. You could tell he could do anything he wanted with them. But never the same one two times."

I wanted to ask him about Samantha Kelly Young, with her curly blonde hair and her pendant that formed the Japanese letters for *sky*. But how would Gideon remember one particular girl? The way Gid drank, he was lucky to remember his way home, and he lived upstairs.

"Do you know his dad?" My voice was almost too quiet for me to hear, much less Gid.

"He's a very nice man. The mother was even nicer. My dad played American Legion ball with Steve in the summers when they were young. And I guess Steve and Merry met young. Merry taught music at the school for a while. She was a dancer. I guess she majored in music before she was a nurse."

"Did you know about the accident?"

Gideon glanced around to see if Angela was nearby. "I was the one who saw it, right after it happened. I was driving home that night with my mother, from a big dance at a relatives' house. We stopped, but my mother made us go on to town and get the fire department. You could tell there was nothing that could be done for poor Merry."

I pressed him. "And what about Garrett?"

"He was standing there. Hands in his pockets. He was looking at his mother like it was interesting to him. I think that was when I first got the idea something was missing there."

I gathered my big sweater closer around me. If only the mother I imagined Gideon's mother to be—a great strong brave bear of a woman, like Gid—would have grabbed that little girl from her car seat before they'd sped away for help. It would have been the wrong thing to do, in every way, in the first aid sense. But maybe she would have been alive today.

Still, was that possible, even for Tabor? Was his own little sister his first victim?

Gideon added, "And I never should have sold him that land."

"What land?"

"Where he's building his 'ski school.'" Gid made air quotes with his thick fingers. "He's supposedly been building it for five years, and it's been ten years since I sold him the property, but when I go out there, all I ever see is a light on up in his boink pad . . ." He looked up. "I'm sorry, Allie. He has a big chalet, and apparently, he just uses the bottom for storage, because he's always up there in the loft part with some chickie."

I was having a hard time breathing. "How do you know?"

"I've got eyes, don't I?" Gideon smiled slowly. "I got binocs, too."

"Where is it?"

"Out by my dad's house, the house where I stay during summers."

"Where the teepee is?"

"Right. You guys stayed there that one night. Yes, where I have my teepee. Up on the south ridge of Lutsen Mountain, the soft ridge. You know where I mean. His land is about a mile before my dad's old place. Under the ridge. There's a good logging track that goes up slow. You can see it right from Cannon Road." He managed a sad smile. "Allie, I know you and Rob and Juliet skied out there."

"We did, but when we stayed in the teepee, Rob's dad drove us up there. Why did we only come one time? That was the coolest night ever. I'm trying to place it . . ."

"If you think of looking over the left shoulder of Torch Mountain . . ."

"Oh! I know now." And I did. The trails that circled that part of Lutsen Mountain were too gentle to be much fun on anything except cross-country skis, but they made cross-country a little bit more of an adventure. The three of us had gone there a few times. "There aren't many houses out there."

"That's because it's either tribal land or Gideon land."

Angela was back, and had nestled next to me in the booth. Her eyes were drooping. It was after ten o'clock. Some good big sister, me.

"Could I use your boat?" I asked Gideon. The plan had formed in my mind before I could even form the words.

"Going fishing?"

"No, I left something out in the lake the other night," I said, and it was a measure of Gid's character that he didn't ask what I'd accidentally left on Lake Superior in January. He only nodded. I said, "Can I use your truck, too?"

"Be hard to pull the boat without the truck." Gid paused. "When do you want to use it? I have to go get it."

"Tonight? Tomorrow? The next day?" I had clinic tests tomorrow, for the experimental trials.

"I'll leave it out back. Wednesday."

Rob would be back on Thursday.

That was good. If he couldn't answer my phone calls, or my texts, or anything, I would . . . I would show him how much I could do without the help of anyone. I was Allie Kim, just as I had told Garrett Tabor, so long ago. I was Allie Kim, the Great and Terrible. Juliet used to have *G.T.* tattooed just below her hipbone. She said it was what the other skiers called her, Juliet, the Great and Terrible. Although I knew now what those letters really stood for, I still thought of her that way.

Once, years before, Angela asked me if there was a beforeward, like there was an afterward. I know that she meant. If I had known "beforeward" what the afterward of my borrowing Gid's boat and his truck, would I have done it? It's human nature to make loops in our minds. The yes-loop. The no-loop. The of-course-not-loop. Most of the time, both of the loops twist and turn and wind up the same place.

It wouldn't have made any difference.

I missed Rob terribly, was the truth. I was displacing pounds of grief with pounds of pizza, and pounds of fear with pounds of anger. I had lifted a flap on the corner of my mind and peeked at what it would be like to miss him forever. When I did that, I thought, *How could such a thing ever be possible?*

Anything is possible.

I said, "Thank you, Gid."

With his help, I threw Angela over my shoulder, fire-carry style, to take her out to the car. I really only intended to go tether the Odyssey—if, *oh please*, it was still there.

I never meant to do anything else.

19

APART TOGETHER
APART TOGETHER

The next day, I went to the clinic for a battery of tests that were repeats of tests I'd had a month earlier.

Usually, I had my clockwork-timed medical workup four times a year: blood and tissue taken and some various kinds of whateverograms to chart the progress of my condition or the lack of progress of my condition. When I went to the clinic, I saw the same nurses I'd seen for fifteen years, including my godmother Gina. And everybody acted the same way. Everyone slapped fists with me and gave me things.

I still really do like getting things. It's one of the prerogatives that attaches to the shared belief that you will die young and miss some of the allotted birthday presents.

That day, I put on my full level-five biohazard regalia to go to the clinic. I started with long underwear because it was three degrees outside. Then I put on a turtleneck and sweats, long socks and tall boots, with gloves and a bandana with a hat meant to protect the necks of people studying mosquitoes in the Amazon. This, and sunglasses that cost about four hundred dollars, and an umbrella, is what I always have to wear to walk from my mother's car to the clinic door and from the clinic door to my mother's car, whether in record summer heat or the dead of a Minnesota winter. People who don't know me roll up their car windows because they think I must be the Pied Piper for killer bees.

There was no reason even to ask why they couldn't just look at the blood I'd had in my veins thirty days earlier.

With anything medical, it's best to do it three times and bill for it four times. Even then, you could walk in carrying your severed arm and the intake specialist would ask for your insurance card and politely offer to help you get out of your backpack, given that you had only one arm and the other was spurting arterial blood.

"Ginger!" said Gina.

It was my clinic nickname, in reference to the auburn color of my hair—although the texture of my hair and the shape of my eyes are clearly Asian. My mother describes me as "Eurasian," but that makes it sound like I'm on a poster for tourism in Thailand. People expect "Asian" to be little and size zero. But Chinese people are not always little and delicate. On the other hand, Japanese people tend to be the ones who get the kind of XP that leaves you blind and with an IQ of 50 by the time you're ten years old. So XP-wise, I drew the better genetic Asian card.

Gina disappeared behind the sprawling, bean-shaped countertop and came back with a Macy's bag. She had not given me anything in about three weeks. With a conspiratorial smile, she pulled out a little purse with about sixty zippers and pockets, the size of a paperback. I smiled, but I have to admit, I was annoyed in general. Despite my hope and joy over the prospect of not having to wear the killer bee gear—or at least less of it, at least someday, at least maybe—I was still a kid. I was pissed off about having not only all the blood draws and skin slides and mouth swabs and vision-field tests I'd just had in November, all over again, plus an MRI and a bunch of other procedures I hadn't had for years.

I was also fiercely hungry. Gina brought me a bran muffin. "Great," I said. "What a treat."

"It's better than nothing."

"Not much."

"You're welcome," Gina said.

"Gina, Gina," I said. "Is my mom just over the rainbow here? What do *you* think of this clinical trial?"

"Forget about it; I think it's the most promising thing in years," she said in fluent Brooklyn. "I'm telling you, Al, it's the most promising thing ever."

So I offered myself up to be bled and scraped and imaged. When the technicians and nurses took away my blood and tissue and pictures, I sat madly paging through the kinds of celebretrash magazines that my mom would not allow in our house, because there are always one or four tests that need to be repeated. This time it was the MRI, which made me want to scream. I ditched the beheaded remains of the bran muffin in the trash. Everything in a hospital that looks clean is really swarming with MRSA germs. You can get sick standing there. All of the tests took seven hours, and that was just the first battery.

I got home in the early afternoon. I was ready to hit the bed when my mother asked, "Why is Rob Dorn sending me text messages?"

I was too tired to lie. "I wrecked my phone while I was taking pictures, and I could not get to it, and it's totaled," I said. "I'm sorry, but that is what happened."

"You need to go to the store right now then, and you need to replace it."

"It's not dark out."

"I didn't lose the phone, Allie."

"Mom, you don't want me to go outside except to go to the clinic under pain of death! You can't be two kinds of drill sergeant."

She relented, and I collapsed on my mattress waking vaguely to notice that there was a new phone, unboxed, under my hand. Well, that was why we paid for the protection.

Relieved that Rob had texted me back, no matter what he'd texted, I hit the bed seriously.

When I woke up, I sent a text immediately: I love you. All is forgiven.

And he answered, immediately: I love you too but I really was texting your mother. I know we need 2 talk but busy now.

And so I texted Rob: I am going to find out where he hides what he does. I do not need you. FU very much.

And then I fell asleep.

My rhythms were a mess, because I woke up twelve hours later, early the next afternoon. Turning in bed, I reached out for my bottle of knockout pills, took one, and was out again.

THE HOT, SAVORY smell of veggie chili woke me. Ravenous, having eaten nothing since the previous morning, I jumped up with fuzzy teeth, rumpled hair, wearing a Notre Dame sweatshirt with a big hole in the elbow over pink long underwear. Rob was standing in the kitchen with my mom, eating a mug of chili.

"Hi," he said.

"Hi. You came home early."

Rob set the chili down.

"I missed my girl. You're still my girl, right?"

I blinked. "Of course. If you want me to be."

"I thought about nothing but you for all those days. Allie, I love you so much. It would be better if we broke up. But I love you so much."

"Why would it be better if we broke up?"

"It just would. You're starting college . . . and all."

Again, I had the strong sense that the "and all" was missing, but I decided not to push it. "I'm going to brush my teeth before I give you a kiss," I said.

"It's okay. You look like a Doctor Seuss drawing."

"That's what every girl dreams of a guy saying." I toddled off to the bathroom, and then turned back. "Did you get my text?"

"That was why I came back. The last thing you said, honey, that's not happening."

"You broke up with me. You don't get to call the shots anymore." I put my hand up and touched the chain under my sweatshirt. The ring was there, but so was the pendant that had belonged to the lost girl.

"Allie, don't be like this. This is what started it before."

I stared at my mother, who had made no move to give the two of us space to have what was clearly a very private discussion. She shrugged and hustled Angela upstairs. I could imagine the two of them hanging over the balcony like bats to hear us better.

"Come with me to get my parents tomorrow night. They stayed until the last day with my mom's brother. Come on." He took a step toward me. "You're not wearing it."

I pulled out the chain.

"So that's how it is," Rob said, glancing at both of the charms on my necklace.

"That's how it is," I said, my voice thick in my throat. I turned to go brush my teeth. When I came out of the bathroom, he was gone.

I waited an hour, and then, on my new phone, I texted: At least be happy about the clinical trials!

An hour later, he wrote back: I can't be in them.

Why not????

Wrong kind of XP, he wrote.

I wanted to run after him, then. I wanted to put my arms around him and say it was just a matter of time—months, not years—before they figured out the key to his kind. Instead, I asked him to let me take him out to dinner the next night, before he picked his parents up, at a nice place, The Flying Fish—which was the only place still open in Iron Harbor, that at least we could talk.

Good, Rob wrote.

But it wasn't.

20

SILENT CONFESSION
SILENT CONFESSION

We were finishing our chicken parm when I finally asked Rob, "Are you sure?"

It had been such a sweet night, just us two, pretending that things were the way they'd once been. I hated to get down to cases, but I was never patient, and I had to know. He understood right away.

"About the clinical thing? Yes. Bet your butt. Your mom checked it out before she told me."

"Jackie told you?"

"She's a good person, Allie. Why would she not tell me? You've always known, I have it worse than you," he said.

It was a fact, and not one I wanted reiterated, although I had asked for it. Rob had already had a baby melanoma removed, leaving a gnawed-looking pouch of scar on his shoulder. I knew then that there were plenty of things he wasn't going to say, no matter what, and would I change that?

No. I looked over at him, at his slender white hands and

his black curls, his dark and deep-set eyes. Rob was Rob. I wouldn't change anything about him.

"Are you going to be angry with me because I'm having gene therapy or whatever it is?"

"Like I don't want you to live and be healthy? How would you be if the situation were reversed, honey?"

"Jealous. But . . . happy it was one of us."

All at once, Rob wasn't looking at me anymore. He was intently watching something just over my head, outside the little curtained cubicle where we sat. The Flying Fish is a sort of combo Italian-seafood place. It's meant to be romantic (at least for Iron Harbor), and there are six or eight raised, scooped little booths, nestled against poofy banquettes, with cove ceilings and plaster angels and velvet drapes across them for people who want to make out in public but not be seen. We'd done that in the past, but I got the distinct feeling we weren't going to now.

Barely opening his lips, Rob said, "Don't move, Allie. And don't speak too loud."

"Why?"

"I can see Garrett Tabor and his father across the restaurant. But they can't see us. I wish I could hear them. They're having a fight."

My heart thumping, I slowly turned my head and peered through the break in the drawn red drapes. Rob was right. Oblivious, their nearly identical profiles rigid, the two Tabors were hissing at each other. They were animated, with ugly gestures and expressions, but deliberately keeping their voices low. "They can't be talking about anything personal," I said. "They're in a public place."

"That's what we were just doing," Rob pointed out. "If only you had that camera."

"I do," I admitted, pulling it out of my front pack. "What are you going to do with it?"

"We can't hear them, but we can record them," Rob said. I was so proud of him at that moment; I wanted to leap across the table and sweep him into my arms. Rob could have just pulled the curtains tighter. Instead, he knew that I would want to know what my sort-of boss was talking about to my sort-of murderer. I hadn't even told Rob about my solo dive, because I figured it would outrage his protective-guy instincts. But they were already there, and they were already wrapped around me. Slowly turning the volume up on the camera, making sure the lens was jutting out to just the correct angle, Rob put his fingers to his lips and pressed the RECORD button.

Just then, the server breezed in and said, "Does anybody here want dessert? Want to just look at the menu?"

Furiously, like mutes, we nodded our heads, and she set the card between us and backed away. Before she could exit, Rob touched her forearm, pointed to tiramisu, and made a sign for "two."

A moment later, she returned with cups of the thick, creamy dessert, waving her hand at us as though she couldn't speak either.

Rob continued to record. At one point, I heard Dr. Stephen say, distinctly, "What I did!"

But the rest of it was muffled, the sound of distant voices. The two men got up, and Garrett Tabor threw down some bills and stalked out of the restaurant. After a moment, Dr. Stephen added another bill and left, quietly.

I almost laughed. On top of everything else, Tabor was cheap, too.

✧ ✧ ✧ ✧ ✧

WHEN WE GOT back to Rob's apartment over the garage, he hooked up the camera to his biggest computer and uploaded two minutes of video. It consisted mostly of a close shot of Dr. Stephen's face. We could see him shake his head, spread both hands in anger or despair, and I could even lip-read well enough to see that he whipsered, "No! No!" on three occasions.

"We don't know anything from this," I said to Rob. "And I have to leave. I have to go get something."

"Go get what?"

"Honey, if I was going to be in any danger, I would tell you. It's just something I left in the woods the other night when I had the camera out there."

"Don't go near him without me, Allie," he warned.

"I promise." Most of what I was telling Rob was true. Technically, Lake Superior was in the woods—or at least part of it was. "What should we do with this film?" I asked.

"We're going to give this to your FBI agent," Rob said. "I'm emailing it to you right now."

"He's my professor. He just used to be an FBI agent."

"But he's connected. He knew about the voiceprints of the phone calls from Juliet. He knows about this, too. Someone he knows is an expert in this stuff."

I shook my head. "We couldn't get lucky enough that they're talking about anything real in a restaurant. Maybe he's just mad at Tabor for some ordinary thing."

"Why would the father of an adult get that mad? It's not like he took the car without permission."

I almost laughed again. "That's probably exactly what he did. He took that Lamborghini without permission."

"No. Look how upset Dr. Stephen is. He's furious. If Garrett Tabor really is who he says he is, Dr. Stephen wouldn't have anything to be that upset about. His son is successful and has respect and a nice girlfriend. A bunch of them. So what's wrong?"

I sighed, even though I was secretly reveling in the fact that Rob was just as committed as I was now. "It could be anything. Maybe he thinks it's cheesy that Tabor sleeps around so much. When you open up people's personal lives, it's not like their public lives."

"That's exactly what I'm hoping," Rob said.

"If I was going to say something about a crime, I wouldn't do it in front of who knows who."

"It's just like you said, Allie. The restaurant could be camouflage. No one's listening to them. I bet this conversation wasn't planned."

We watched as Dr. Stephen gripped his temples with both hands and looked out into the restaurant. If he had been able to think straight, he might have seen us. Rob was right. Dr. Stephen didn't look angry in an ordinary way. He looked personally aggrieved. He looked as though he'd been assaulted. I thought again of the photos that had come while Rob was away.

I called them up.

"This is sick. He was watching you," Rob said, staring at the screen. His already pale skin turned a shade whiter. "We don't know how many times."

"That's what scared me. Not even my mom knows what was down there when we dived. I'm too afraid that if I tell her, he'll find out. Then, before I can do anything . . . he'll get them. He'll get my mother or Angela."

"But be reasonable, Allie. How could he get hold of them or hurt either of them without anyone suspecting . . . ?"

"You know that. Remember Nicola? Remember my

friend? No one even knew there was another car on the road the night she went off the bridge. And her only crime was seeing me see *him* with Juliet at the Fire Festival."

Rob gave me a cold glare. "Why didn't you tell me about these pictures he sent?"

"I would have! It was while you weren't speaking to me, dummy! I tried to call you eight times one day."

Rob shrugged. He pulled me close to him, his mouth tasting of rum and cinnamon. For the next hour or so, we even managed to forget about Garrett Tabor.

WHEN I SAT up, it was after eleven. Wesley might still be out west with his "lady," but I was responsible for that boat. "Drive me to my house," I said to Rob. "Come on. Hurry."

When we got downstairs, we were puzzled about why it was so difficult to open the door to the driveway from the stairs. It was as though someone had wedged a weight against it. Finally, using our combined strength we pushed it open and saw that a foot of snow had already fallen. From the way it was coming down, we were in for the kind of epic Minnesota blizzard that makes people believe in vengeful deities. I wouldn't be getting any boat tonight.

Fretting, I called Gideon at the restaurant.

He chuckled. "Oh, you mean the little rubber inflatable. I already brought the rubber dinghy up to shore. I put it in a circle of rocks and covered it with a tarp. I saw your fins washed up, and there was a plastic box in it with your phone in it." He paused, and I heard the tinkling of ice in a glass. "Allie, the fins are okay but I think your phone has had it."

"Gid, how did you even know I was going after a boat?"

"What else would you be going out on a lake for? And why would you need a boat as big as mine?"

"Gid, thank you." I thought of him patiently hauling up the anchors and putting the Odyssey back to shore, probably having to pole through a crust of ice at the edges of the beach to bring it up, then standing in the freezing cold, hatless, winching his own boat out of the water. "You saw my fins? On the rocks?"

"I saw your buddy, on the rocks." The spark went out of his voice. There was another tinkle. "I yelled for him, but he was looking for something. When I got over there, I saw one of those extra long blue fins, and the other was already washed up on the beach."

"My buddy," I spat. "Well, he lives there, in that penthouse."

"It's for sale."

"Gideon?" I said. I walked back up to Rob's door, as he struggled to shovel out his Jeep, and closed it lightly behind me. "Could I still use your truck?"

"I'll leave it in your driveway," he said. "Be careful. Driving, I mean."

"I will."

Months ago, Rob and I had speculated: Was it remotely possible that Dr. Stephen knew about Garrett Tabor? How could you know such things and protect the person, even if he was your child? I squeezed my eyes shut, remembering my best friend. How could you protect that person if he was your lover? Juliet was afraid he would hurt me or Angela if she didn't do what he said. Yet until the very end, that night at the bridge, I know that a part of Juliet had still trusted Garrett Tabor, despite everything.

People could believe any version they wanted to, if they wanted to badly enough.

❖ ❖ ❖ ❖ ❖

DESPITE ROB'S DILIGENCE at trying to get the car out, no one was going anywhere in snow that was now two feet deep. Snow always stops everything—even the bad stuff of life—and it's like a small psychological vacation. I couldn't leave Rob's. This made us feel entirely adult. Rob's parents left us scrupulously alone when we were in his garage-top quarters. But we'd never been as truly alone as we were tonight. So we snuggled in to watch the Arctic blast through the huge glass panel Rob's dad had installed across one whole peak of the roof. Letting nature have sway was fun. However, I'd forgotten, until I glanced at the clock on the TV, that Rob had obligations. It was after midnight. His parents were supposed be in Minneapolis at 6 A.M. He would need to gear up and let his father take over once he got there, because the roads were going to be slow.

"Maybe I'm missing something. Do you think your parents know about this storm?" I asked him.

"You're kidding, right?" Rob said. "All my dad does is travel. He has a chip in his head."

"What?"

"My dad checks the weather like it was his heartbeat. My parents already called. And they have no idea when the airport out there will open, and the airport here sure isn't going to be open tomorrow. Everything's shut down."

I said, "I love you."

He said, "Well, Allie. I love you, too."

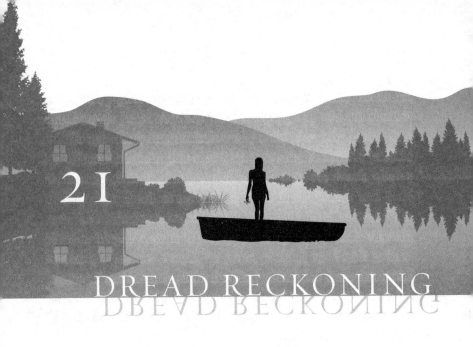

21

DREAD RECKONING
DREAD RECKONING

I t was two days before the semester began, and he was certainly harried, but Dr. Yashida not only answered my email promptly, he answered with a phone call.

"I have been thinking about you and your welfare," he said. "You are an original student already."

I didn't know whether to thank him or be embarrassed. But I told him that there was another favor I needed to ask of him.

"Can someone tell what someone is saying by just seeing him talk instead of hearing him?"

"Most of the time, the machine really is hearing the person. You can enhance it."

"Is there any way you could try with a file I have? It's very important, and I'm sorry to intrude."

"That's okay. Is this urgent?" he asked.

I said it was, extremely.

Curiously, Dr. Yashida didn't seem surprised, almost as if he'd been waiting for me to enlist his services. It was one of those moments I once had when I was stoned with Juliet, when you think you're part of the steering column of some BMW driven by Venusians, when it seems possible that every-thing is a mirror and everything is a replica of a replica.

HALF AN HOUR later, Dr. Yashida wrote to ask if he had permission to pass along our video to two analysts. One of them would enhance the quality of the recording and take out any accidental noise. Another could glean what Dr. Stephen was saying by reading his lips, a criminal forensic special-ist—like the kind I would be one day. The analyst was deaf. Lip-reading was both her job skill and her life skill. It was the worst sort of reverse prejudice, but her disability made me feel more confident in her.

It was helpful, Dr. Yashida wrote, that our subject was a clear speaker. It was possible for the analyst to see most of what he said. He asked for a name. I said it was Dr. Stephen. No last name.

Later that day, a message came in, with the transcript.

> *Dr. Stephen: No! No, I can't.*
> *Other speaker: (Unintelligible) oh problems.*
> *(Long period of street noise, as a plow or some other maintenance vehicle passes)*
> *Dr. Stephen: (Unintelligible) a felony. A state crime. And a federal crime. (Unintelligble) I believe you. I don't believe (Unintelligible) you did, Gary. It could (unintel-ligible) anyone (unintelligible) good life. A good life.*
> *Other speaker: Eye or I (Unintelligible) . . . wrong way or day.*
> *Dr. Stephen: Of course. Yes, I am guilty.*
> *Other speaker: (Unintelligible) . . . win no hope . . . who she is.*

Dr. Stephen: I'm not sure what to do. (Unintelligible) water in her lungs. She did drown.

Other speaker. Accidents do (Unintelligible). This was . . . accident. No one . . .

Dr. Stephen: I can't do that. No. No! No. That much I can do, and I should, Gary. I did what I did.

Other speaker. Sorry you feel that way. You think that I did (Unintelligible).

Dr. Stephen: No. I'm not saying that. Of course I do. She was a kid.

Other speaker. All ways. You. You all ways . . . do?

Dr. Stephen. I am not sure what to do. (Unintelligible) Your team. Yes, I would. No! No. It's not possible.

(Long period of garble, as other diners take a table, talk among themselves, meet the server and then move to a larger table.)

Other speaker: Impossible (Unintelligible) no hope for me. (Unintelligible).

Dr. Stephen: I'm not sure, Gary. You have a good night. I will see you . . . Gary?

A note from Dr. Yashida arrived after I thanked him.

He asked me to let him know if there was more news about this incident or my friend, and he urged me to take these messages and the report of the voice analysis immediately to the nearest office of the Minnesota Bureau of Investigation. He was a close friend of an agent named Molly Eldredge whose specialty was serious crime.

Fear can't be your motivation here, Allie, he wrote. *As you're learning, fear among individuals is what the bad guys count on.*

If I would give him permission, he would share everything with her now, and someone would have a conversation with Tabor.

Rob and I read the transcript again and again. We were stunned.

We watched the video.

"He's talking about Juliet, isn't he?" Rob finally said. "Could he be?"

"He has to be. He's saying he covered up that she died from drowning."

"I'm not sure he's saying that."

"He seems to be."

Rob shook his head. "I don't think I can make myself believe that he would do that. Does it mean he knows about Garrett Tabor and Juliet?"

I thought of what Tommy had once said to me and Juliet: if you can think of it, someone has already done it.

"This town is their empire, Rob. It's like they are the barons who live on the hill and we are the serfs. I can't believe someone would cover up anything like that. But what if she was already dead and he didn't want his son implicated in her death?"

We thought back to the night that Juliet jumped from the bridge, how urgent she was and how unprepared. I remembered how Rob and I, in the center of the bridge, both believed we had heard her land on the bank of the creek bed. Only then did we hear a scream and a splash. A few days after her funeral—for reasons we now recognized more as needing proof than needing closure—we had done the jump ourselves. Even though it was long, and diagonal, both of us had landed with room to spare.

"Juliet wouldn't have drowned," Rob said.

22

CLOSING IN

Taking Rob's Jeep, I ran home to get some clothes. The forecast was for snow, but the forecast is always for snow in the North Woods, from Labor Day onward. In all those nights outside, I'd tried to train myself to smell snow coming, and sometimes I could. I brought a toothbrush in case. With Rob back in my arms, and with the new evidence to ponder, I didn't want to leave his side. I rifled through my drawers as Angela pouted in the doorway.

"I do not want the babysitter," she said.

"But I have to go out."

"You didn't go out for two weeks! That was better. It's boring when you go out. Kissing, kissing, kissing. Doesn't your mouth get sore?" In fact, it was sore. "Can't you stay home just tonight?"

"I can't tonight. I'll be home more when I'm in college. I'll have to be here all the time at night because I have classes on Skype."

"I hate Mrs. Staples," Angie said.

"You don't really. You hate that she's not Mom or me."

"My life is so awful! I just come home and do home-work and eat some disgusting stuff and go to bed. That's all my life is."

"You're starting dance class," I offered.

"Big deal. Who wants to come home, do homework, eat some disgusting stuff, and go to boring dance class and go to bed while you never see your only mother and sister?"

She did have a point.

"What do you want to do, Angie?"

"I want to be a skier. Like Juliet. I decided at Christmas. Something happened this year, and I became a very good skier."

On the plus side, she couldn't have gotten much worse. Our videos of Angie falling off the rails last year were manda-tory sharing with mom's family. Her rear end had personally wiped most of Torch Mountain.

"I want to learn to jump," she said. "And Coach Gary will teach me."

I had been folding up some pretty underwear Mom had given me as a Christmas gift. I froze. I had to look at my hands and say to them, *Open your fingers. Lay the clothes down.*

"How do you know Coach Gary?"

"He came to our school. He showed videos of Juliet, and he had me come up and talk about her because she was my best friend who was practically grown up. And he showed videos of Barrett and Ben." These were the Ebersol twins, who now skied for the Canadian team. "He told me that it was better that I was shorter, like Juliet, and that he could teach me. I can sign up for classes."

I stared at her. "You can't go around Garrett Tabor, Angela."

"Thanks! You don't like him because he thinks I would be good at something and you want me to come home from school, do my homework, eat some disgusting . . ."

"No," I nearly shouted. "You can't talk to him because he's a bad man."

"How's he bad?"

There was no truth like the real truth. I took a deep breath.

"Rob and I think that he hurt Juliet once. We think he forced her to have sex when she was just in freshman year. Do you know what forcing someone to have sex means?"

Angela nodded furiously, her eyes deep and wide. Of course she did: Jackie Kim would not have neglected good and bad touching with a nine-and-a-half-year-old fashionista who favored bikinis with boyshorts.

"We think he may have hurt Juliet when she disappeared," I added.

"But he's, like, Mom's age."

"It doesn't matter. He's bad."

Angela's eyes went full saucer. "He killed Juliet?"

"I don't know. But if you hurt someone, unless you're trying to protect your child or your sister or something, that means you broke the law, or you are crazy. And he knows I know this. So he sends me things that prove he could hurt you. Like bad teasing."

She leaned against the door frame, her face twisting in a scowl. "He acts so nice!"

"You can't tell Keely."

"I know," Angela said, quietly. "Because he might hurt Keely, too." It touched me that it didn't occur to her for a moment to doubt me.

"Does he do things like hanging a doll in a tree?"

What shit was this?

My head spun dizzily. "Yes, like that. Did you ever see a doll hanging in a tree?"

"Yes."

"Where, Angie?" I gasped. "Why didn't you tell me?"

"I wasn't supposed to see it."

"But you have to tell me, anytime you see something weird or scary like that. You have to tell Mom or me right away."

"I wasn't supposed to be watching the show."

Never had I felt greater relief over my sister's clandestine wish to avail herself of inappropriate entertainment choices. Neither Jackie nor I could figure out how to install the parental controls that the satellite dish said was a snap to use. (Without a dish, TV in Iron Harbor was like good radio). Three hours into trying to make it work, with a pleasant-faced spokesguy telling us the whole time that anyone could navigate this system, Jackie threw the monitor at the screen, which cost her thirty bucks for a new monitor. At the time, she muttered, "I don't care if she watches Real Showgirls of Las Vegas live."

A few moments later, Angie said, "I taught Mrs. Staples to make ice cream."

"Good," I said. "Listen to me. I won't leave you too many more nights."

He really was supernatural. He was everywhere. He was the chess master. He owned the board.

Grabbing up my things was the moment I later realized that I'd set my course. He might have owned the board, but I would checkmate him. He had to be stopped, and no one would do that except me.

23

DARK STARS

R ob dropped me off before eleven that night.
Neither of us felt like doing much talking.

Rob didn't even make the pretense.

Either he didn't notice Gideon's truck parked in the shadows of our driveway, or he didn't care. He seemed distant, preoccupied. What Gideon called a "thaw wind" was blowing off the lake—and that lovely, isolating, pristine snow was sliding off roofs in great heaps. In the darkness, I could barely see Rob's face, but he looked tired, as though we hadn't spent most of the past two days lying in bed, resting and dozing.

"What's the matter?" I asked.

"Nothing. Thinking maybe. Schoolwork I didn't do, and junk. My parents will be in at two A.M. Their flight was taking off at ten P.M., but they already knew it would be delayed. Everything's backed up. But I have to scoot."

"Well, bye. Let me know what happens before you go to bed."

"Lucky first day at school."

"That's not until the day after tomorrow."

"Oh."

"I got from five to nine five nights a week and Skype a class on Saturday morning from eight to ten. It'll be great."

"Hmmmm."

"It's a class in being naked. All the students are naked. Even the professor is naked."

"That's good," Rob said.

"Did you hear me?"

"See you, Allie."

He drove off.

I stood in the driveway for a moment, wondering if the conversation I'd just had with Rob had actually taken place, or if it was some surreal nightmare. Then I rushed for my house, punching in the combinations for our locks and security system. Mrs. Staples was asleep and snoring on the couch. She sputtered, sat up, sat down again, and pulled down the hem of her maxi-length wool skirt. "You're home, Allie. I was expecting your mom."

"And she'll be right here. I have to go back out, Mrs. Staples. Is Angela asleep?"

"For hours. School tires her out. Fourth grade is the hardest one. I always thought that with my boys. Fourth grade, seventh grade, and junior year. And she had her new dance class tonight for the first time." Angela and Keely were taking hip-hop at the YMCA.

"Did she like it?" I asked, planning the architecture of a double Brie and pimento with romaine on wheat toast.

"She said she did."

In my room, I slipped into my featherweight black waterproof pants, then I sealed up my sandwich, stuffed a few cookies into a plastic bag and filled my Nalgene with ice water. I put the kettle on, so I could bring a thermos of tea. While it was boiling, I plugged the camera into the charger, stuck my phone on the dock. After that I hefted my old poles out onto the porch and slid into my fuzziest boots and the no-nonsense parka that drawstringed at the waist and the butt. Long fingerless mittens with suede palm pads and little hoods to shield your fingertips when you didn't need to use your phone: *check*. For my head, Juliet's real mink hat with the silly red-and-green knitted bobble strings (I tried not to think about who had given it to her). The teakettle boiled (would I ever hear a kettle boil without thinking of Blondie?), and I spooned some honey into the thermos with a couple of tea bags before pouring boiling water over all of it. My miner's light on its headband (with fresh batteries) and my Maglite. A long scarf that I could wrap triple. And then, the big flat-headed screw-driver that was really a kit, and had all those other attachments inside: one of last year's Christmas gifts from Angela to our mother. Finally: the filet knife Rob had given me when I caught a six-pound smallmouth bass.

Into my little backpack went all of it.

Then I was out the door, standing on my toes to slip my skis and poles into Gid's truck bed and hauling myself up into the high seat with the bag filled with gear. At the last moment, listening to some primal cue, I ran back into the house and grabbed a blanket. Back up, four feet off the ground on those fat tires. But after I turned the ignition, I hesitated. With the truck rumbling, I hopped back down again.

"I'm sorry, Mrs. Staples. My mom will be here any minute!" I said as I breezed in the door.

"Slow down, Allie! You'll leave your head on the counter next!"

Not exactly what I wanted to hear.

I ran into my bedroom and sent an urgent-marked email to Professor Yashida.

Dear Dr. Yashida,

This is from Alexis Kim. I want to give you per-mission to share whatever Rob Dorn and I have given you with whomever you knew in the Minnesota Bureau of Investigation or any other Bureau of Inves-tigation. The person doing most of the speaking in the video is Dr. STEPHEN TABOR, Iron County Medi-cal Examiner.. The other person is his son, GARRETT TABOR, ski coach, school board member, registered nurse, and genetic researcher. Last fall, I saw Garrett Tabor with a young woman who was my best friend, and who I now believe is dead. I believe that Garrett Tabor is responsible for the disappearance and death of JULIET LEE SIROCCO. Thank you for your help and kindness.

I attached newspaper clippings about Juliet's disappear-ance, although I'd already sent them to him at the time of the voiceprints.

Then, I left, merrily calling back some nonsense over my shoulder. As far as Mrs. Staples knew, I was now off to my life as a teenager without a care in the world, probably meeting up with her beau for some moonlight picnic.

If only.

I had never driven anything bigger than my mother's Toy-ota minivan, so it took a moment to get used to the sheer heft of the truck. But soon, I was cruising along Beach Road toward the back of Lutsen Mountain, not letting myself think, not letting myself plan, trying only to observe and stay in that very moment. It was just after midnight, not far past the south end of town, when the high beams of Gideon's truck picked up the sign for Cannon Road. I didn't go up here much. As Gideon said, most of the land was tribal or private. Some of the older "motels" that were located on part of this mountain had reverted to their rightful owners (the tribes) after fifty-year leases ran out. While some had been bulldozed, the majority just sat there in mute, foolish anticipation of families with kids in swimsuits who would never come back. Beheaded charcoal grills and snaggly shutters underscored the atmosphere of abandonment. The fronts of the old motels seemed to watch you, their broken windows like old eyes, swiveling to follow your progress. They were good places to make campfires and have a sit-down if you were on a long night's ski, but I found them eerie, not antique enough to be beguiling, but instead creepy the way some old black-and-white movies were creepy. When I passed one, I could see evidence that someone had used the place as a squatter's refuge. There was a wreck of an abandoned very defunct car, its hood up and its motor cavity filled with snow, and a heap of trash in front of Unit 11 at the Trail's End Traveler's Inn. The sign unfortunately featured an image of "The End of the Trail": Minnesota artist's James Earle Fraser's depiction of a defeated warrior on horseback, head hung low. (Fraser was also, I remembered bizarrely, the creator of the Buffalo nickel image.) There was A Summer Place, an entire building clad in Pepto-Bismol pink, and a little farther on, The Pines, a two-story Cape Cod building that once had a restaurant promising "The Finest Fish Fry in the North Woods."

In time, the former resorts vanished.

In the broad glow from the brights, the snowfields smoothed out, broad pectorals and concave abs like a goddess lying on her back. Here and there was a summer home, shel-tered under the nanny cluster of tall pines or thrust out on a short cliff. These places were lush, and motion lights picked me up, hundreds of yards away. While lamplight burned in a couple of windows, I didn't think there were people asleep in there. The way up was steep, but Gideon's truck was more than a match for it. I imagined Rob and I fishtailing around in his Jeep on this road, already mushy, as the temperature was on the rise. I drove slowly, stopping periodically to shine my light over what appeared to be breaks in the snow, looking for the well-worn fire track that Gideon had described.

I was in the right place. I could see the summit of Torch Mountain and the lighted windows of the Timbers a little to my right and in front of me, to the north, its gondolas glit-tering in the darkness like a slow-swaying string of bright beads. There were a couple of what seemed to be driveways or snowmobile tracks with dark, hunched buildings at the terminus—and these would probably have been hunting cabins of some kind. About half a mile farther on, the road crested and widened, flattening out.

And there it was. The wide track swept away from Can-non Road, and in the distance, I could see faint lights from some kind of big house. I turned into the road, slowly, and stopped, first opening the window and then killing the engine.

This was the place to get out.

With every part of my body, I did not want to abandon the safety of that big Dodge truck, with Gid's implied presence. But this was as far as I could go without being detected. If anyone were to be up there, if this was even the right place . . .

Backing out, I drove another mile, to where the road bucked up again, and cinched on itself back toward the front of the mountain. Gideon's summerhouse was up there;

I knew that much. When Rob and Juliet and I were about twelve, we'd spent a night camping in Gideon's teepee. It was everything a genuine teepee should be—hide-made, thirty feet in diameter at the base, rising to a height of eighteen feet on tall lodge poles, with a neat fire ring and thick log benches as comfortable as any mattress. That would have been the spot, then, I thought, if Gid's directions were right. Gid's wife at the time (number two or three) had brought us big plates of venison stew and fry bread, which tastes like what they would feed you every morning in heaven. At the urging of Gideon's wife (why had he divorced that one, Kerry or Cherry? She was nice! She'd probably divorced him . . .) we sat at the base of a tree until the animals all around believed that we were landscape. In time, a grey fox led her huge-eyed kits around our feet, so boldly that one of the tiny pups rolled right over Juliet's leg. Deer and their gawky, spotted babies came out into the meadow, where Gideon had a big salt block. Despite having grown up with these animals all around us, their proximity, in that setting, was thrilling.

Usually, kids who camp out stay up all night.

But after we'd seen the animals, we couldn't resist the combination of our sleeping bags and those grooved, satiny log benches. A single ghost story from Gideon's wife—about a woman who had run her white Cadillac off the road at eighty miles an hour, and who appeared on dark nights in the road to help other drivers do the same thing—and we were out until the song of Gideon's flute merged with the song of birds waking in the trees around us.

That night changed me.

A few summers later, I began taking Angela on moonlight picnics. We took leftovers, or just a bag of trail mix: food was never the point. We had seen things together that only people who lived in the dark could ever see. The art of still-ness was something that I had learned in a CT scanner, in an examining room, in hours alone, at age eight and nine and ten, wondering what other kids were doing in the sunlight and why I could never be with them. I convinced Angela to try stillness when she was so small it was almost impossible for her to do. By the time she was in school, she was so good at it that she could eavesdrop on almost anyone. One night, a timid, gigantic moose cow crossed before us, with her spin-dle-legged calf. A fish eagle dived just before dawn to feed her enormous, wobble-headed chicks. We lay on our backs, and I made up stories about the constellations. I didn't tell the traditional myths, but stories of two sisters, one who would shine in the morning and one who would shine in the night, and how they met in the middle.

"I'm the shine-at-night sister," said the seven-year-old Angela. "When I grow up, I'm going to stay up all night."

"When you grow up, maybe I'll be able to come out in the sun. Maybe I'll get better."

Last summer, when we'd taken a picnic, nine-year-old Angela looked away from me, studiously, sharply, her thick brows drawn down in a scowl. "I'm going to be the only sister," she said. "When I'm grown up, you'll be dead. That's what happens to people with XP."

"Yes, I know. That is true. But I hope not."

"That's what Keely says to me. That you'll die soon."

That I would die soon was something that Angela should not have had to pace her way through, every day of her life. But the odds were good that one day, she would have to say goodbye to me, much sooner than was justified. Jackie and I had opted not to tell Angela about the gene therapy trials until there was something to really tell.

Angela!

What was I doing out here after midnight, gathering up strands of my old life just as my new life—with the hope of a cure for XP and the life of a college student—were literally rising in front of me?

How could I pull something like this on my mother?

What did I think, that I could surprise Garrett Tabor in his lair? Find him sifting through skeletons and smack him down with my big screwdriver? Jackie would be home now, not suspecting that I was anywhere except with Rob. I glanced down at my phone. If there could be negative bars, I would find them here. People who lived out this way must have satellite dishes mounted on poles seventy feet tall.

I was Allie Kim, not the Great and Terrible, but the small and meek.

Still, I off-roaded Gideon's truck into a thicket of trees so as to go unnoticed. I nearly screamed when the thing promptly sank into a drift so deep it would make opening the driver's side door a challenge. I was a Minnesota girl, adept at rocking cars, but this was beyond me. The truck was mired beyond rocking and would require tow-truck intervention. Well. I had my skis. I couldn't be more than five or six (or eight) miles from my house. I would ski on over and see what was there, in that soft cluster of lights, and then I would ski back home and confess my wickednesses to Gideon via a phone message. I would offer to pay for the tow. I knew he would refuse. I hadn't hurt the truck in any way, at least. Before I left the rapidly cooling warmth of the cab, I suited myself up for a ski, regretfully leaving my boots behind in the cab and slipping on a pair of extra wool socks under my cross-country boots. With any luck, I could pull myself from the cab into the bed of the pickup truck without having to drench myself in the drift. Somehow, I stuffed the thermos into that backpack and wadded the little blanket in around it. I hadn't fallen on skis since I was ten, but there could be a first time. Picturing myself on this road waiting out the night with a sprained ankle did not make for pretty daydreams. After the night would come the morning, and those images were even less attractive. I could burrow into pine needles under the blanket, but that warmth wouldn't last as long as the protection. I'd have a nice-looking frozen corpse.

I looked down at my watch. It was after two. I was running out of night.

Enough.

Standing on the running board, I swung myself easily over in the dry cab, secured my skis, and easily traversed the drift. In case he should come looking for me, or for his truck, I left Gid's keys on the antenna, strung from their rawhide lanyard.

I adjusted my miner's lamp on my head but didn't turn it on. It was too warm for Juliet's hat, although it was in the pack. Most of the failures in my brief life, I'd observed, were failures of patience. So I stood in the dark until I could make out—by the light of the moon that had emerged from behind shreds of clouds—the track, the trees, the distant outlines of some kind of structure. And then I took off, in easy glides that soon felt like doing nothing. If I were going off on a fool's errand at least it helped to be strong-legged and aerobically unassailable.

No more than twenty minutes later, though, my skis were almost useless. I was on gravel, unsure what lay to the left and right of me. It looked like snow-glazed dirt. I thought of my boots, back in the cab of the truck.

Allie, there's always a way to screw up, I said to myself.

Well, I could try to break some kind of trail.

It was like skiing on black ice. Slippery and nearly impossible. I didn't know how much time had passed until I looked at my watch. It was just a few minutes after three.

Closer now, I could see the building Gideon had described. A massive chalet, its most beautiful feature was a wide floor porch that wrapped around the second story. The first floor looked to be taken up half with a garage and half with some kind of pretty glassed-in room that wouldn't be in use this time of year. I studied the lights. One glowed in a lushly paneled room on the second floor. I took out my camera and peered through the telephoto lens. I could see the décor—dark red couches and chairs, blond wood moldings, a big fireplace of brick and stone. There were overhead lights, dim, recessed, in that room. To the left and right were other rooms, but someone had drawn blinds over those sliding doors. I imagined a plush bedroom or two, and a big kitchen.

Nothing stirred. The light gleamed still and steady.

With a starling plop, a big dollop of snow hit the ground right behind me. To this day, I wonder why I didn't think, where did that come from? I wasn't standing next to a tree . . .

He was a nurse, after all, and nurses know all of your places. With two firm fingers and a knowledge of the nervous system, a nurse—or even a social worker—can take someone down who's three times the person's size and strung out on anything from love to uppers. I wasn't strung out at all. That was what Tabor did with me. A slight pressure on my shoulder, and I went sprawling, before I could resist, and by the time I could get the use of my arms and legs back and start kicking, he had dragged me to a steel door and pulled it open, shoving me into that garage—into the windowless, stinking dark.

"You don't listen, do you Allie?" he said.

I knew he couldn't see in the dark any better than I could. So I said nothing. I let my backpack fall to the floor and made sure I knew where the outside pockets were.

"By the time your pal the drunk shows up, the fumes from this little thingamajig I've got here will have killed you. I'd like to say it's been nice knowing you, and it was fun for a while, but now, it's just too much trouble. Although . . ." He squatted down close to me. "I could stay for a few minutes if you were nice to me." I could smell his breath, meaty and minty. "Maybe you can live if you're nice. But you can't keep your mouth shut, can you Allie?"

He slid his body up next to me, grabbing the mitten off my left hand and putting my warm palm on his lower thigh. Blue jeans. My right arm was stronger.

I let my left hand go limp and Tabor inched it up his thigh. That was where I stabbed him.

"*You bitch!*" he screamed.

He was up and out the door before I could react and wedge something in it. It didn't snap closed automatically, because of the drift of the snow. But it was on some kind of spring, and it began rapidly to eat the column of paler darkness. Shucking my remaining ski, I jumped to my feet and tried to jam it into the door. I pushed my shoulder against it. It must have been six inches thick. I could hear Tabor outside, swearing and muttering as he made for the car I'd evidently missed.

He couldn't have been hurt too badly, not unless I got lucky and hit an artery.

I kneeled near the doorway trying to get my hands around the edge of the door before it slammed. But I was too slow, and I fell away in defeat. At least Tabor hadn't been able to turn on some engine or propane or whatever he'd said he had. Maybe he never had anything at all.

All I had to do was bundle up . . . and wait. I collapsed back, pushing myself away from the door that was colder than the meadow outside.

Then I heard the clank and slither, behind me. I smelled the foulness in the air—an animal smell that had nothing to do with cars or gas.

It was quicker than I was.

I stood, but before I could jump to one side, it sprang and jerked me down, by my shoulder and my hair.

24

ZOMBIE ANGEL
ZOMBIE ANGEL

"Bear? Did I hurt you? I couldn't let you leave without me. I should have let you go . . ."

I was crying before I could speak. I reached out with both hands to pull her to me. In the darkness, we fell on some kind of thin rug. I held my Juliet, what there was left of her. For minutes, that was enough. She stank of dirty hair and wounds and messes that had never been cleaned.

I'm a pristine person. I held her closer. I wouldn't have cared if she were radioactive.

Finally I whispered "Is it really you?"

"It's really me. Bear, I'm so sorry."

"Sorry. No. Don't be sorry. Did he hurt you?"

"I'm not hurt. I did everything wrong. I did everything wrong."

"You've been here all this time?"

"Since the night I threw boiling water on him in his penthouse. I convinced him I wanted to make tea . . . he thought I still believed him, about Bolivia. If I didn't go, he said he would wait until you were out driving with Angela, and then—"

"I know."

"So I took a hot shower . . . and I let the towel fall off around me . . ." She breathed in, and I could hear the rattling in her chest. She was sick. But she would get better. I willed it so. "That makes me want to throw up now. Oh, Allie!"

"It's okay, Juliet. It's okay! I promise. I'm here now."

"He was always going to bring me here. He had it all fitted out for me. My mattress where he rapes me. The hole in the pipe where I have to hang onto a strap while I pee. The bowls for the water and soup he pushes in here with a pole I can't grab. Just bowls of water and soup. Like a dog. No spoons. No . . . toothbrush. I used soap on a rag to wash my mouth. And this." She put my hand around the slender length of steel links around her waist. It was fitted with a harness of padded leather, so that the chain wouldn't hurt her. Or ever let her go beyond its length.

I reached up for my headlamp. No luck. It was somewhere on the ground outside.

But I had my Maglite. Throwing the pack on the floor, I rummaged for it, and pulled it out. My heart galloping, I turned it on. Juliet blinked and shied. Her blonde hair had grown out, chin length, with rusty maroon tips where the dye job had been. No one had ever given her a comb. Her face was covered with scrapes. There were sores above her upper lip. She was unspeakably befouled, grimy and emaciated. But it was Juliet, the real Juliet. I wished I could send my thoughts to Juliet's mother. *Be at peace. Hold on. I'm bringing her home.* Juliet smiled. All her perfect teeth, undamaged by more than two months in this prison, gleamed. That body was never hers. Whose was it? Dr. Stephen had lied. Somehow, someone had matched samples of Juliet's tissue with a girl who died, another way. Dr. Stephen knew about his son.

Rage boiled inside me, overcoming fear. He knew, and he knew this place was here. Dr. Stephen Tabor, the Iron County Medical Examiner, and with Dr. Andrew the leading authority of XP research in the world, knew that the body we buried wasn't the daughter of the Iron County Sheriff.

Garrett Tabor could not let us out of here.

What was he going to do?

I had her, here, alive.

For how long?

An odd disconnect between the real and the movie version billowed forth in the room.

My best friend, my heart, my other soul—and more, the key to the ultimate proof of all Garrett Tabor's concealed atrocities, to Dr. Stephen's lies about the poor nameless girl whose ashes we scattered as Juliet's—was right here. Trapped. I was dumbfounded, numb. How could we escape? The ghost of me, the younger me, the Allie-Bear-me, leaped from my Alexis-planful-body and back again. She needed me now. I needed to think of a way out.

"Here is hot tea with honey," I said. I watched as Juliet's filthy hands grasped the thermos. Greedily, she drank. "Probably not so fast."

"Can't help it," she gasped. "He starved me. His plan was my periods would stop, but he didn't want to kill me." She turned her big, upside-down blue eyes on me. "Allie. Is my mother . . . ?"

"She's okay, Juliet. She's not okay. But she can get better. Tommy, too." I paused, about to unwrap the sandwich. "Can you hear what's going on out there?"

"You can. If he started his truck, we would have heard it."

"So he's coming back?"

"How bad did you hurt him?"

I thought for a moment. My knife slid deep into his flesh, but had I been able to damage muscle? Vein?

"He could be doing first aid on himself," Juliet said softly. "He's not worried that we'll get out of here. There's no way out of here. That door is flush in the wall. If I lie down on my stomach, I can almost touch the door. But not completely."

"How could a nurse let you get so sick?"

"He likes me this way. He likes me to depend on him. He would wash me before he did things to me. And there's a medical box in here. He would sometimes fix them up after he raped them. He brought them here, and he set up a light, so they could see me."

"Who?"

"The girls."

I shuddered. I forced myself to repeat the word. "Girls."

"Not little girls. Not like Angela, but like us. Or a little younger. Or a little older." Scuttling back, Juliet began to pull small bits of paper from a crack in the wall. "He left a pencil here once. I wrote everything down. I don't know if anyone can ever read it. I made marks for every day. I thought of you every day. And every time I knew there was a girl. Five of them. One of them had a baby of her own. She told me when he left us here alone here in the dark. When he wanted me to sleep, he fed me pudding with drugs in it. I ate it because I was too hungry to refuse, even though I could smell something in it. I didn't care if he was poisoning me, even. When I woke up, that woman with the baby, she was gone."

"Where were they from?"

"He picked them up in nightclubs in the Twin Cities. He

picked them up at ski resorts. The woman with the baby was the oldest, almost his age. She . . . they're dead, Bear."

"How do you know?"

"I said, I can hear things from upstairs and outside. A little. Too much." Juliet breathed in. Again, that horrible rattling. She had pneumonia. "Do you think you hurt him bad?"

"I don't know."

We sat quietly. I swung the light around the room. There was a steel sink and a pile of clean rags. I walked over and stuffed one against the faucet, but when I turned it on, there was an enormous banging in the pipes as the water burst out.

"What if he hears that?" I whispered, leaping across the room to huddle with Juliet.

"There's nothing we can do. He'll either come back or he won't."

"What was he talking about, gas?"

Juliet pointed to a propane cylinder, lying on its side, and a plastic red jug of gasoline.

"He said he would turn that on, and we'd die from the fumes. I didn't believe him because the cold gets in here. It's not airtight in here. If he set fire to it, he'd burn down his whole place. So I didn't believe him." She lifted a trembling torn nail to her lip. I pulled it down and began gently to wash her face. "I hope you hurt him enough that he doesn't come back."

I remembered then that I had the big flat-head screwdriver.

Quickly, I studied the way the door opened . . . in, and from left to right. There would be plenty of room for me behind the door if Tabor opened it. He wouldn't expect me to have another weapon. The screwdriver was actually a screwdriver set, with a bunch of different heads in the handle. The handle probably weighed three pounds. "Don't worry," I said. "If he opens the door . . ." I held up the screwdriver. "I won't stop hitting him." Juliet nodded. I saw her eyes swivel toward the door. "Were the phone messages from you?" I asked.

"Yes," she said. "The first night."

"You screamed."

"When I screamed, it was because he burned me." She pulled up the loose cuffs of the hospital scrubs she wore over waffle cloth long underwear that must once have been light blue. Then, she held out her arms. There, I could see two identical scars striped along her biceps. "He used an art tool. Like you have when you're a little kid with a wood-burning set."

I winced. Juliet lay against me, her breathing a loud wheeze, and began to talk. She talked about hearing music and laughter and the snap of high heels on the floors above. Then thumps too loud to be anything except someone falling. Sharp and broken screams. Muffled sounds of something striking flesh. She told me about Garrett Tabor's hammer, a special mallet covered in padded leather: he never liked a mess. I broke my sandwich up into bits and fed her small chunks until she said she couldn't hold anymore. Juliet couldn't have weighed more than eighty pounds: at her biggest, Juliet, who was only five foot two, weighed a hundred and five. Without realizing I was doing it, I was rocking her, as I once rocked Angela.

"It's okay now. We're going to get out. Either way and whatever happens, we're going to get out. Gideon gave me his truck. That's how I got here."

"How did you find it?"

"Gid sold him this land. He talked about seeing him here

with girls. Last night, I didn't think I would find you . . ."
Had I? Had I thought I would find at least proof that she was
truly dead or alive? "I thought I could find something that
would nail him forever. So I was going to pull Gid's truck off
the road, but it got stuck. I skied up. He grabbed me."

"So Gideon knows you're here."

"Not that I'm here. He knows I have his truck."

"So . . . sometime. Soon."

A thought was pinwheeling around the back of my head.
What if Tabor just didn't care? What if he got a bandage on
and was ready to take off? What if he came back in here and
didn't give a damn what happened to this house? What if
he planned to spread the gas around and throw a match in?
He'd be on a plane by the time the fire was out. Juliet and I
wouldn't live through it. If he was as smart as I thought he
was, if he had that nearly supernatural ability to derive the
scene and to plan ahead, he probably had money cached in
places. He probably had other identities, passports. It wasn't
hard to get another passport, if you got the birth certificate of
a baby who had been born around the time you were born.
It didn't even matter if the baby had died. You could go to a
cemetery and pick out a new person to be. I would have to
fight him with whatever I had, but he already knew I had a
knife. I walked over and picked up the propane cylinder. A
piece of that in the face and he'd go down. I would use whatever it took. All I needed was a little warning. And a whole
lifetime's worth of courage.

"It would be better if we got out of here fast."

"Look," Juliet said. "It's morning. You can see a line of
light." She was right. There was a seam at the edge of the door
that wasn't quite tight. If the "chalet" was under the brow of
the mountain, on the south slope, then the sun was already

up on the other side. I pulled out my non-viable phone. It was shortly before seven in the morning. How long had I been in this place? Three hours or more?

"If he hasn't come back by now . . ."

At that moment, a big motor roared. There was a sharp shout, then a babble of voices, all shouting. We heard the muffled sound of running. Something smacked hard against the door. Backing against the far wall, Juliet and I took refuge under my blanket. I inhaled the smell of Jackie's chlorine-free, corrosive-chemical-free detergent, as though it could bring my mother to me through the molecules on the fabric she had touched.

Then there was an amplified shout. I heard the word "Stop!" and then again, "Stop!"

Then shots.

Three shots.

Someone was banging on the door.

"Open up! Open up! Federal officers!"

"We can't open the door!" Throwing off the blanket, I ran to the other side of the thick metal barrier. "This is Allie Kim. I am in here, and you can't open this door without warning me. I have XP. Juliet Sirocco is alive. She is in here with me. She has XP."

"Allie?" said a familiar voice, a woman's voice. "Hang on. Hang on."

We heard the approach of the sirens, then booted running feet. Many dozens of feet.

"I'm going to come in, Allie. With the firefighters. You stay covered. They're going to use a blowtorch on this lock. I'll bring in protective gear for you and Juliet, and the ambulances will have blackouts for you." The voice said, "Move him."

I fumbled for my sunglasses and wrapped my scarf around

my face. I pulled my hat and gloves on over my hair, reaching out to cover Juliet with her filthy sleeping bag and the blanket I'd brought from my house.

When the door fell open, in the small seconds it took before the paramedics covered me, I saw the black glisten of blood on the dusting of snow outside the door and Garrett Tabor, facedown a few feet away against the wall. The back of his parka was pristine, but the ground below his was soaked.

In the other direction, medics were bent over a second still form. Jeans. The orange and blue of a Chicago Bears caped throwback jacket.

The doors slapped shut

"Where is he?"

"He won't ever hurt you again," said my doctor, Bonnie. What the hell was Bonnie doing in the ambulance with me? "He won't ever hurt anyone again, Allie. He's dead."

"Where's Rob?" I said then. "I meant, was that Rob?"

"The medics have him, honey."

I screamed, "It's light outside!"

Bonnie tapped the window between the back and the driver. She said, "Go."

IN THE END

Why people at the hospital insisted on examining me, I had no idea.

I was fine. I was never better.

All I wanted was to get to Rob, to make sure he wasn't burned, and to find out about Juliet. I wanted to make sure that my mother called Tommy and Ginny.

What I didn't get was that there was something much larger going on all around me, something I couldn't quite make sense of.

My mother was waiting for the ambulance and ran next to the rolling cot they insisted on putting me on. "Mom, I'm not hurt!" I said.

"I know."

"I'm not even cold."

"I know," she said. "You were right all along. Allie, you were right and you didn't tell me. You didn't tell me about him."

"He threatened you and Angie."

My mother held me close against her. "He threatened my little girl. You. I'm glad he's dead, Allie. He might have gotten away. He might have gotten out of prison. I'm glad he's dead and in Hell. Oh, Allie. I can't believe you went through this alone."

With my mother beside me, a doctor and two nurses whisked me into a darkroom.

I said, "Does Tommy know?"

"Yes," Jackie said, smoothing my hair. "Yes. Tommy knows. Ginny and Tommy are here with her."

"Is she dying?"

"No," Jackie said. "I looked at her myself, sweetheart. She's malnourished and she might have bronchitis. She's fine, Allie. She's fine. You saved her. Rob . . ."

"Rob?"

"Rob saved her," my mom said.

"Where is Rob now? Mom?"

Bonnie entered the examining room. She exchanged a glance with my mother. I frowned. She was dressed in a long, dark green padded coat, brown boots, and an olive-green suit.

"Who killed Garrett Tabor?" I said to her.

"I did," Bonnie told me quietly.

"Where's your gun?" I said.

"In my locker. I don't carry it in the hospital."

"I thought you always had to be ready. Semper fi."

"I'm not a Marine, Allie."

"You're something."

Her face softened. "I'm retired from the Air Force. I went to medical school in the Air Force. I was recruited by the bureau, by the FBI, while I was in the Air Force. Willingly. I wanted to go after guys like Tabor. I trained in psychiatry as well as general medicine. And I was an abused wife. My husband was a good dad. He was a horrible husband."

As to the answer to the big question—why Bonnie hadn't told me—of course, I knew. I wasn't a Navy Seal. If I had known that Bonnie was an FBI agent, and Garrett Tabor had threatened me, or Rob, I'd have sung like a canary, the way they say in the old movies.

"You were safer not knowing. Allie, I had no idea what would happen tonight. I'd been trying to track Tabor to wherever he hid things for a long time. That was why I came to Iron Harbor from Chicago last year. That was why I came to work at the clinic, and at the medical examiner's office."

I said, "Are you really a doctor?"

"Of course I am. Lots of FBI agents are doctors or lawyers."

"So you really don't have to save for tuition for Chris and Elliott."

"Sure I do, sweetie . . . I'm just a federal employee, Allie. I'm not on *The X-Files!*"

I rubbed my eyes, feeling very tired all of a sudden. "What happened?"

"Tabor was on his way out of here. Rob literally, physically ran into him at the airport. Rob left his parents as they were headed for the baggage claim. They just got up here now. They had to rent a car. Rob chased Tabor back up to his place. Tabor zigzagged all over the place, which is how I found out about it, because a local sheriff's deputy saw him, but he IDed the truck as Tabor's and didn't bother to stop him."

"So by the time Rob followed him up here . . ."

"He ditched the truck on Cannon Road."

"Rob followed him . . . his tracks," I said.

Bonnie nodded. My mom hugged me tighter. "Rob couldn't get the Jeep up here. He followed Tabor on foot. But Tabor didn't know Rob was following him."

That was why we hadn't heard a car engine start. Tabor's own big truck was miles down the hill. How long had it taken Tabor to get up there, only to find me in his front yard? An hour? More? Tabor was in great shape, but so was Rob. They would both have been tired, but it was nothing except a long walk on wet ground. Tabor, Bonnie went on, tended to his business in his house. Rob waited, hidden, outside in the yard. Tabor stayed inside for two hours. When he finally came out, Rob tackled him, and Tabor couldn't get away because I had done some damage with my filet knife. Meanwhile, Bonnie had gone up there alone, but when she saw Tabor's car, and the extra set of tire tracks, she called for help. Sheriff's deputies came first. But by the time she was on scene, there was another agent—Molly Eldredge, from the Minnesota Bureau of Investigation. Her old teacher, Barry Yashida, had been in touch with some odd and compelling information when she, coincidentally, got word of Bonnie's plan to apprehend Garrett Tabor.

"I never knew that Rob would go out into the sunlight . . ." Bonnie said.

I stiffened. "Rob was in the sunlight? Mom?"

"He's in the ER right now, Allie. You couldn't see him anyway. Even his parents can't see him. He was burned, but nobody knows how badly. Just wait now—"

"I have to go where Rob is!" I shook free of her embrace.

"Allie. I said you have to wait. This is a medical reality. Not a suggestion I'm making."

On my feet, pacing, I turned back to Bonnie. The nurses tried to get one of my hands to measure my heartbeat, but I brushed them off.

"There was no way to tell Rob?" I asked her. "You didn't warn him?"

"You can't get a phone call in there, Allie. I tried to call Rob a dozen times," she said. "I would never have wanted him to be hurt in any way. You know that." I did know that. "I'd never had any luck with it coming together with Garrett Tabor. It was what his father said in front of you and Rob that gave us a reason to even talk to him. It was just luck, Allie. Sometimes luck is all we get."

"But you knew that Juliet was . . ."

"No, that is not true!" For the first time since I'd known her, Bonnie looked truly angry. I know she felt horrible. "You can't think I'd let an innocent girl suffer to catch any criminal, no matter how vile that criminal was."

"She does know that," Jackie said.

"We just didn't have all the pieces, Allie. He was very clever."

"You killed him. You didn't ask questions."

"Allie, I called for him to stop. I fired a warning shot. I told him again to stop, and I identified myself. Garrett Tabor returned fire. He had a shotgun, and I have a Glock twenty-two-caliber pistol. I shot him."

My mother glanced down at her phone. "Allie, Rob is on the medical floor now. Because of infection, they would not ordinarily let you see him. But because of . . . other things, if you put on clean surgical garments and wash up, you can see him."

"Where are they? The surgical clothes? Will you teach me how to scrub in?"

She did.

26

THE LOVE YOU TAKE

THE LOVE YOU TAKE

It took half an hour for me to be clean, my nails clipped and scraped, my hair washed and under a surgical cap. When I got down to the floor where Rob was, the Dorns were waiting in the hall. I looked up to smile as I passed them.

Mrs. Dorn's eyes were slits in flesh rubbed as raw as a child's from crying.

"It's not your fault, it's her fault," Mrs. Dorn said, sharply. "She should never have gotten involved with that man."

I thought of Juliet's face, the first time I saw her alive since I'd assumed she was dead: the blue eyes in her filthy face, terrified and yet desperate for the sight of me, the mess around the pipe, the bowls that were never washed. I thought back to the night that Rob and I were locked out of his car at daybreak, and that was no accident; it was Tabor all over. I saw again Juliet, in a wheelchair, her leg stitched up, coming . . . now I recalled . . . into this very room. We huddled together in the bed, eating a bag of cheesy popcorn, Juliet's favorite, as she confided for the first time the full truth of her old history and her new terror of Garrett Tabor. It was then that she vowed to me. *Never again, Allie Bear. Never, ever again.* And yet, at least so I assumed, she had gone back to him. That was the reason for all her agitation on the night at Lost Warrior Bridge—the reason for her frantic and fervent goodbye. Even then, at the last moment, she must have thought she had some power over him. She must have thought that she could seduce him away from hurting me. She was afraid of him, but she was still willing to do that.

Juliet had made mistakes. But she was just as brave as Rob.

Until last night, a part of me thought Tabor had guaranteed Juliet a passage to freedom and she had literally jumped for it. Now I knew, he had guaranteed her a passage to hell.

I said, "No, Mrs. Dorn. She was just a kid. She was at his mercy."

"From what Rob said, she was a kid who learned pretty quickly."

"Not that he was capable of murder. Juliet was a good girl."

"She was a good girl? She was a *good girl*?" Mrs. Dorn eyes were all pupils, dark and dreary. "Do you have no idea at all what went on here? Are you clueless? She was with a man twice her age!"

"I am not clueless. I know what Juliet did. But she wasn't wrong. She was a child who was forced."

"She was always showing off," Mrs. Dorn said.

"The reason she ended up out there was that Tabor said if she didn't come with him, he would hurt her, me, or my little sister. Rob was so sick of hearing about Garrett Tabor that we broke up over it . . ."

"But he couldn't stay away from you. Or forget her."

My throat tightened. "Rob loves me, and we've been best

friends all our lives. The three of us. Would you blame any other rape victim? One who didn't know Rob?"

"Yes, I would," Mrs. Dorn spit the words out. "If it wasn't for her, Rob wouldn't have gone out there."

"Stop now," Mr. Dorn said. "My wife, Rob's mom . . . she's out of her mind."

"I know," I said.

"See if you're proud of Juliet after you see my son," Mrs. Dorn hissed.

"I'll always be proud of Juliet. I'll always be proud of Rob. I love Rob."

Still, at the door, I recoiled. If Rob's backpack hadn't been sitting in the corner, in a big chair, I would not have known him.

He looked like a monster.

Huge blisters dripped from the distorted shape of his beautiful square chin and his forehead, and his eyelids were so swollen they bulged over the patches of gauze on his eyes. His head was bandaged above the hairline. His strong torso was unmarked, because he had worn a layer of silk under a layer of flannel, so that he wouldn't need more than a warm-up coat . . . but his hands were grotesque, bulging and bluish grey. Lines sprouted from his neck and the inside of his elbows.

I said, "Oh, honey. Oh, Rob! What did you do? What the hell did you do?"

He said, "Come close, Allie."

I did.

"I thought I could stop him," he said.

"Bonnie told me. You shouldn't have done it." For a long time, I simply sat there, while Rob woke and slept. The medicine they'd put in the bags seemed to soothe his restless movements.

Mr. and Mrs. Dorn, wearing protective clothing over their regular things, came into the room. I could hear her behind me, crying harder at the sight of Rob. He woke to the sound.

"It didn't make any difference, Mom. It didn't matter." His voice was a dry croak.

"How can you say that? You're hurt! You're badly hurt!"

"Allie knew he was hiding something," Rob said. "She always knew. I wanted to ignore it. If I hadn't listened to her, Juliet would still be out there." He turned to me, or at least in my direction. *His eyes! They might be permanently damaged*, I thought. But even that would be an acceptable trade for keeping him. Was there a chance that I wouldn't? "Allie, are you there?"

"I'm right here." I didn't want to touch him, for fear I would hurt him more.

His voice slipping with the effects of the medicine, Rob slipped one of his big, swollen hands around my small one, like a helmet. He asked, "Did Bonnie get him?"

"Yes," I said.

"I suspected that Bonnie was FBI," Rob said. "I thought, why is she so into this? I saw her take him down. And I have to say, for something that awful, it was pretty damned magnificent. Will he live? Will he have to tell about everything he did?"

"No," I said. "She said he had a gun. I guess she had to shoot to kill."

"Wow," Rob said. He was still a boy, not yet eighteen.

"Rest now," said Rob's mom.

"She needs to know everything."

"She can come back," said Mrs. Dorn. "We need to be with you now." She turned to me, her face nothing like the Mrs. Dorn I knew, always perfectly made-up and composed.

Tall and slender and fashionable, Mrs. Dorn had always looked like one of those moms who would stay young forever. Now, she was stooped, and her hair hung in strings. She didn't look slender, but, like Rob, skinny. I couldn't help but imagine how my own mother would be if I was the one here. Her only baby lay gravely wounded. How little it must have meant that his girlfriend needed him, too.

"I'm sorry," I said to her. "I'm so sorry."

She softened then, and put one arm around my shoulders, giving me a little hug. Although Mr. Dorn was the bluff and friendly guy, everybody's buddy, Mrs. Dorn had always treated me with respect. Since we were little, we had trooped in and out of Rob's house, literally like vacuums sucking up homemade food, scattering the plates, making noise, dumping sports equipment, banging around to loud music. So it was gentle, finally, when she spoke up. "Allie, you need to understand something." She put herself between Rob and me.

"I can tell her myself," Rob said.

"Then do, Rob," she said, her face a new sheet of tears.

"Leave us alone, then, okay, Mom?"

With Mr. Dorn, she left the room. I felt the page of something turning, and I didn't want it to.

"Allie," Rob said. "I'm dying."

27

IN REAL LIFE

In movies, I would have dropped to my knees. I would have screamed and thrashed until someone gave me a sedative. Mercifully, a drape of forgetfulness would have fallen across that moment, until I could better cope with the certain agony that I was losing my first true love, the only boy I could ever love, and that there would be no happy ending. The thought of Juliet, alive and with me, was no consolation. I had outlived Juliet, and I knew I could outlive Rob, and months from now, laugh again. But I would never be the same. I was too young for outliving.

"Why now?" I asked.

But I already knew. Rob did have it worse than I did, and he'd had narrow escapes before in his not-quite-eighteen years.

When you are this sick, denial is not only your friend, it's your only ally. Every night, you wake up prepared to deny that your sight might be a little dimmer, or your hearing a little less acute, that you skin isn't mottled in a funny way or the ends of your fingertips aren't really a tiny bit numb. With all your might, you try to be like everyone else, when you really are like no one else. The only person you're like is the person who has XP, too, the person closest to you—who is just like you, and whom you will lose if you don't die first. Juliet had been that person for me, and then Rob and Juliet had been that person for me, and then Rob and I fell in love, and we were like one person—except that sometimes, I stopped in my tracks to admire the boy who loved me. It was almost worth having XP to have someone know you so completely.

No one ever could again. Some XP people were with Daytimers. But I didn't see how they could be.

Rob said, "Do you believe in Heaven?"

I wanted to say that I did. But Rob *did* know me completely. Just as I had known, honestly, even before Juliet disappeared, that he was keeping something from me (your only ally is denial) he would have heard the lie. In my voice I said, "No, honey, I think this is all."

"Well, then this has been my Heaven."

He wasn't a boy who talked like that. I didn't feel brave. The beauty in his words just made it all worse.

"Mine, too," I said.

"If I could live a hundred years more, there would only be remembering the first time I touched you, remember? Kissing you in the parking garage? When I knew I loved you."

"Rob, why is this happening now?"

"The melanoma came back . . ."

"There are things they can do . . ."

"And I've done them all, Allie."

He was telling the truth.

In real life, I knew that my beautiful, hunky big man weighed twenty pounds less than he had last summer. I had seen that, but I had not wanted to see that. In real life, I saw that he was always tired and paler than the way people like us are pale. I had not wanted to see that, and pretended it was nothing but anxiety. The truth was I had grown stronger, physically and in my deep core.

Rob, instead, had withered. Always game, always ready for the next adventure, the cautious one but never a follower, he had simply run out of steam.

"You kept this to yourself. You kept this from me and I love you. How, Rob?"

"How could I tell you this?" Rob said. "Allie, I should have told you. I tried to break up with you instead. But when I was away, I realized I was just thinking about me. I needed you to stop thinking about Juliet and Tabor and be there with me, while I had the time. But that's not you, Allie. You couldn't give up on her. You didn't give up on either one of us."

Trying to speak around the sobs that shook me, I said, "How long have you known?"

"Just before Thanksgiving. I knew I didn't feel right. But I didn't know it was like this."

How had I withheld this time from him? How had I let a hundred other preoccupations crowd my mind—from Garrett Tabor's threat to the identity of the dead girl called Sky? Little girl detective jazzy jump-up, I'd lost track of the dearest thing on earth. My best friend. My first love. The boy I would marry someday.

Should I ask him to marry me now?

"The ring you gave me," I said. "Would you marry me? I would love to marry you now."

"It wouldn't be fair."

"Why, Rob?"

"I'd just leave you," he said. I could tell he'd thought about this. I could tell that he wouldn't be moved. "Anyway, I already feel like I'm married to you."

"How can you not be afraid?" I whispered.

"I'm very afraid," Rob said, reaching up to remove the patches over his sightless eyes.

"Should you do that?"

"It doesn't matter. I can see a little light," he said, scanning the ceiling. "I'm not a hero, Allie."

"Does it hurt?"

"No. Not even a little bit."

They had Rob floating on the big opiate air mattress of drugs, the very best. When they don't bring you dental floss, he told me, you know that at least they're not worried about you becoming an addict. I hoped he couldn't see shapes, or movement, because I flinched when he said that. It was so final, so unbelievable, so not what should happen when you're eighteen. And it wasn't lost on me that I'd believed that Rob and I would live our life together remembering Juliet, not Juliet and I remembering Rob—in different ways.

"Does it help for me to be here?"

"Honey, I don't know. I don't know how much I want you to see. Things . . . happen when you die. I'm not like this seventeen-year-old guy. I'm like five, and I have to go to kindergarten alone. I want my Obi-Wan snack sack. I want my mom." I wanted to hold on to him and cry until I was drained, picturing the little Rob, as I had known him, with that very Obi-Wan lunch sack. "Sometimes I want my parents to be like in those documentaries they made us watch in clinic where the parents are holding their kid and saying, 'It's okay, it's okay. You don't have to hang on for us. Just hang on *to* us.' But my mom has nobody. She's an only child. She has no friends. My mom is so scared I can't let go," Rob said. "Allie, you know my dad. This is killing him. He doesn't even have a way to let me go."

"And I am supposed to let you go? I am supposed to know how to do that?" I climbed up beside him, careful not to dislodge all the dressings on his hands and arms. "Make room for me," I said. "Tell me why you did this."

"I knew he had some kind of lair," Rob said, softly, his words slightly slurred by the drip of painkillers. "And he didn't think I would follow him. And I didn't think Bonnie Sommers-Olsen would follow *me*. I didn't see anyone. I never even looked back." Rob drew a long, rattling breath.

"Did that hurt?"

"No, I'm fine."

"Maybe you should be quiet now," I said.

I tried to remember him as he had been. Of course, I had hundreds of pictures and videos of all those years—and would I ever be able to look at them.

Rob was asleep.

Quietly, I beckoned Mrs. Dorn to the door. She came. "What are the doctors saying? How many years? How many months?"

"Weeks," she said. "I don't believe it. He's in such amazing physical shape. He worked out four hours a day, Allie. You know. You all did that once. That's what they say though. His poor organs are shutting down. You can't see how jaundiced he is. He's struggling to breathe, but he won't let them put a breathing tube in."

"Why?"

"He wants to talk to you. And . . . he doesn't want to be held on to . . ."

What did I want to say to this poor woman, this woman

I'd known my whole life. "I'm not a mother. I don't know how you feel. But I love Rob as much as I could ever love anyone. I wanted to spend forever proving that to him. I wish you would not blame me. Because none of this is my fault." I also wished my mother would drop down from the ventilation system, brandishing her sharp tongue, my sword and my shield.

"I don't blame you, Allie," she said. "Don't blame me. This is a day I tried hard not to see coming."

28

FOREVER AND EVER AND NOW

The days stretched out.

I was probably the only scholarship student in history (or so I believed, then) to miss my first week of school. I turned eighteen in a lounge chair at Divine Savior Hospital, a chair that would have passed anywhere else for a medieval torture device. The time I "got" with Rob was the time his parents went home for showers, an hour of sleep, a desultory meal. I clutched tight to every moment of it.

On the third day, dressed in scrubs—looking eerily, remarkably, like herself—Juliet appeared in the doorway.

"I have to see him," she said.

Instantly, Rob, who'd been fast asleep, jerked awake. "Juliet?"

"Buddy," she said. "My amigo. How did you get yourself in this fix?"

"Tanning," he said, barely a whisper, and Juliet cried, silently, crystalline, long tears that traced the rivulets next to her nose and dripped off her chin.

"Come here," Rob said. The room was darkened, and Juliet, who'd been in isolation even from me, until doctors could determine that whatever ailed her was only the consequence of hard treatment and neglect—not STDs, no viral infections. Outside a plastic sealed curtain, her parents spoke with her through a microphone, for hours on end.

Later, Juliet, the duchess of impatience, said she wouldn't have minded if her parents read aloud from the phone book or recited nursery rhymes or recipes. Their voices were like a narcotic, her long dark dreams made serene and secure. That night, her face was clean, and her hair was shorn, its natural dark blonde color. She wore no makeup. So thin, in her hospital tunic and paper pants, she reminded me of old paintings of Joan of Arc.

"I'm here," Juliet said. "I'm right here, Rob."

"Juliet, I didn't believe . . ."

"Don't talk. You are my hero. You are all our hero. I would be dead without you. You are Sir Robert of Dorn, my most gentle knight. I hear you're sick."

His damaged lips trembled. "You know how much."

"But you will always be with us, the *tres compadres*. You gave your life to me, and I will give my life to paying you back."

"Tell me how she looks, Allie."

Juliet shot me a glance of pure terror: He can't see?

"Well, all those curves you used to stare at instead of mine are gone. She's a little matchstick with a blonde faux hawk. But she is beautiful to me." Juliet reached for my hand and for Rob's. For a moment, I closed my own eyes, and I whispered, "Tribe," our old Parkour pledge before every trace. And it was the three of us, together again for the last time.

✧ ✧ ✧ ✧ ✧

WHEN THE DORNS were with Rob, Bonnie asked me to make time to come to her office. As it certainly concerned her as well, Juliet came, too.

"This is the first time I've ever met you face to face, though I'd seen you, of course," Bonnie said. "I feel pretty fortunate to see a genuinely reincarnated person."

"I feel pretty good to be one," Juliet said humbly.

While we'd had entirely enough to handle, Bonnie wanted us, my mother, and the Siroccos to know what was going on at Garrett Tabor's chalet. She had already spoken to our parents.

"The whole area is being excavated," Bonnie said. "After the house is searched and photographed, the contents will be removed. Then it will be dismantled and numbered, piece by piece, as evidence." I could hear the half-truth under the even tone of her voice.

"Just the house?"

Bonnie said, "No. The grounds, too."

Whoever was excavating had found things, bad things. People that Garrett Tabor had taken and killed.

"What did you *find*?" I asked.

She said, "I didn't personally . . ." then stopped and sighed. "A human femur. A human mandible. Small human phalanges. And, well, a skull. They're not from the same person. So far. Very recent."

"Were they buried?" Juliet asked.

"They were just . . . scattered in the woods. Animals had moved the bones around. There had been no apparent attempt to conceal the bodies beyond a covering of leaves or pine needles. We found those mounds of needles."

"How many?" I said.

Bonnie examined her hands. "I'm not sure."

Juliet stared at her hands, nervously twitching in her lap. "I was there. I heard them. Oh, god."

"But there were others. Samantha Kelly Young." I gently tugged the necklace from its familiar place on my chest and unclipped it for Bonnie. Into her hand I surrendered the golden pendant that would help bring Sky back to her family—at least that. From my pack, I extracted the copy of the missing girl poster, in case Bonnie had forgotten. "I will give this to my friend Bruce Minty, of the RCMP," she said. "He will spend time with the Youngs and find out their story and where her story ended."

"What's the RCMP?"

"The Royal Canadian Mounted Police," Bonnie said. "The Youngs knew that Sky died. They were sure of it. But of course, like any family, they want to bring her body home to bury."

"Is there any sign of any other, any other girls out here?"

Bonnie nodded. "There is what appears to be a new and deep pit, machine dug, in the hill far up behind the house." Before I could say more, she told me, "They will open that today." *And they'll find the vanished brides,* I thought. Balling my fists, I nearly struck them against my forehead. How could I have been so terrified, and so slow?

"It wasn't your fault," Bonnie said.

"On the contrary, it was entirely *my* fault," Juliet told her firmly. "If I hadn't been so arrogant, and I had outed him when I first felt that there was something wrong . . ."

"Juliet, you were proven dead. Garrett Tabor's father, Stephen, could be charged with being an accessory to murder after the fact, and he certainly will be charged with concealing evidence of a homicide and falsifying documents pursuant to a homicide." She added, "But I honestly don't believe that

Stephen Tabor understood, until right now, that he was deal-
ing with a homicide."

"The girl in the apartment . . ." I said.

"Dr. Stephen never saw the body of any murdered girl
from any apartment. At least, he is not aware that he ever
saw the body you saw in the apartment."

To my relief, she did not say, what you *thought* you saw
in the apartment. Further, she pointed out, the "silent" video
Rob and I had made on the day of the fair had nothing to
do with any girl in an apartment, dead by bludgeoning or
strangulation. As we had hoped and feared, the (now former) medical examiner and his son were talking about the
girl found hung up against the pilings of a pier, a girl Dr. Stephen had apparently confessed to agents he believed died as
the result of a sexual encounter with Garrett that had "gotten
out of hand." He admitted to covering up the fact that she
had not died of drowning, but that was all that he knew. He
admitted submitting Juliet's tissues, reasoning that Juliet was
dead, in any case. A polygraph confirmed that Dr. Stephen
had no idea that his son had been involved in anything illegal
but had terrible guilt about compromising his professional
ethics and claiming that the dead girl was Juliet Sirocco.

Both of us asked what would happen to Dr. Stephen.

"I don't know," Bonnie said. "If he can convince a jury
that he was trying to save his son from a murder charge,
I suppose he could avoid life in prison. There's no way he
can avoid prison altogether. There's no way he can keep his
license to practice."

"That would be almost sad. Dr. Stephen always seemed
so good," Juliet said. "If what he'd done wasn't so awful . . ."

"And somehow understandable," said Bonnie. "What a
parent will do for a child, there are no limits."

Could my mother do it? My mother wouldn't. Or would
she? My mother . . . loved me more than God, more than the
world.

As I thought this over, Bonnie went on to explain what no
one in Iron Harbor except Garrett Tabor and Bonnie knew:
his résumé as a killer was elaborate, long, and detailed. The
first time he'd killed, from what Bonnie had been able to
determine, Garrett Tabor had been very young, sixteen. A
young girl drowned while swimming at a northern lake with
Andrew and one of his cousins, Dr. Andrew's son. The cousin
had heard a scream and saw the girl struggling. When Garrett Tabor came bobbing to the surface, he told his cousin
to swim for help, that the girl's leg was caught on some lake
weeds. Questions were put to Garrett Tabor, about horseplay
and unsafe swimming behavior, but Tabor insisted he'd tried
to help the girl, finally diving to get her foot free.

There were weeds, but her body was floating freely, face
up, when a group of fishermen with a big bass boat finally
made it to her.

In college at the University of Wisconsin, Garrett Tabor
had a girlfriend, a chemistry prodigy named Dang Song who
went by the nickname Sunny D, who jumped to her death from
a fifth-story balcony at a dorm. She had bruises around her
neck, which a bereft Tabor explained to police were the result
of an earlier attempt to take her own life by hanging. There
were other deaths, including two at a resort area north of Chicago—both girls under seventeen, both dumped nude in water,
neither one dead from drowning.

And those were only the victims that had garnered any
suspicion at all.

Tabor had begun coaching the high school ski team eight
years earlier. Unexplained deaths were in the news at the time

of ski meets in Colorado and New York State on three different occasions. Three girls were found naked and strangled,
covered only by twigs and leaves in wooded areas near the
resorts where the events were held.

"Did anyone talk to Garrett Tabor?" Juliet asked. "How
long ago was this?"

"The last one was three years ago, in New York, near
Whiteface . . ."

"I was there," Juliet said. "Whiteface in Lake Placid was
where I competed for the last time. It was where I fell on my
last jump, in the exhibition."

"You have to tell Agent Molly Eldredge all about this,
Juliet. Every word. Even if you think it's not important."

"It's all in what I wrote down."

"Even what you just said? You're the key to everything.
Think back, to those ski meets. Was he ever absent? Did he
act strangely? Did you ever see him with his clothes in any
way torn . . . ?"

"I was fourteen, Bonnie! The only thing I remember about
Garrett Tabor was how much he asked from me as a skier.
And how much he asked from me in other ways, at night."

Bonnie lowered her eyes. "I know, honey. We have to give
you some time. And whatever he did, he would have done
when all the kids on the ski team were fast asleep. Even you."

It was almost as though he were still alive there, still in
the room, gloating. In fact, Garrett Tabor's body had been
released to his family. In an act of what I now consider
extraordinary naïveté or hubris or denial (or all three), they
were preparing to bury him in Torch Mountain Home Cemetery—next to his mother and his baby sister, Rachel.

That was one incident that Bonnie and I seemed to
decide, with a level look, that did not need to ever be fully

explained. Dr. Stephen had done wrong, but I could not see him as evil. Dr. Andrew and his ancient parents, and Andrew's sons, were innocent. About Rachel, no one need ever know anyone's suspicions.

Idly, as we left, I asked, "Who is the Iron County Medical Examiner? Who did the autopsy on Garrett Tabor?"

Bonnie sighed. "Well, for the very brief future, I am acting in that role. I did it. And I assure you, he is dead. It's over, Allie."

29

WHAT PASSES
FOR GOODBYE

The next day, in the corridor, I stopped a nurse. I wanted her tell me the truth about Rob and the time he had left. Absently, she said, "That's a matter for the doctor."

"Stop. Please have some mercy. I might be here alone with him. I hope I am. I don't want it to be his poor mother. I've never seen anyone die. I don't know what to look for."

The woman hugged her clipboard to her chest and pressed her lips together. "Every hour, his breathing gets slower, do you see that?" I nodded. "It's more of an effort. His lungs are filing up, and this is pneumonia we wouldn't want to treat, because it would only make this terrific kid suffer more."

The words sunk in. "So his breathing will get slower."

"Maybe, at the very end, he'll get agitated, a little. He might seem strong. People do sometimes. That's what they mean about the belief that people see Heaven. I don't know what the real reason is, but right before they die, they're sleeping a lot, but they wake up for short periods. They ask for people who are here or who are dead."

"What's the very end of life like?"

"His nose and his fingers will start to cool off. And there may be a sound in his throat, a kind of rattle or cough. And then, one breath will just be the last one."

I nodded. "If I'm here, what do I do then?"

The nurse glanced around her, to make sure that we were entirely alone. "Don't call anyone," she said. "Don't ring the nurse's bell. Don't panic. A mom or a dad, they'll want to start his heart again, and he's a strong kid. That would be possible. But you don't want to do that."

"No."

"He's played out."

The Dorns lived at the hospital. I went home to change and then I came back, sometime with my mother, sometimes not.

Most of the time, those last three days, Rob slept.

ONE EVENING, MY mother came in with Angela. My little sister looked bewildered and gaudy, her fingernails and toenails painted like watermelons and ice-cream cones. I saw the hand in this of someone in a room down the hall, still on high-calorie shakes and pushed of IV nutrients. Angela was only nine. She couldn't pretend that she didn't think that Rob's life for Juliet's return was a good trade.

Before Mrs. Staples picked her up, Angie asked, "Juliet didn't die, so who did?"

"I don't know," I said. "A girl fell in the water."

"Was she just like Juliet?"

"She was someone's little girl."

"That's not fair."

"No, Angela. It's not fair."

"But we got Juliet back."

"But they didn't," I said. My tone was hard. I couldn't help it. "And I don't know if they'll ever know where their girl is."

"That's what I think," Angela said. "That girl had to die, and Rob had to, so we got Juliet back. Mom says what you say. I say, it has to be a trade. Somebody had to die."

I shook my head. "No, Angela!"

"Yes, somebody did have to die! Now Rob is sick, and he has to die!" Angela was nearly in hysterics. The next moment, she would be screaming. I grabbed her shoulders and dug my hands into her frail arms.

"Stop it, Angela. Most things in the world don't make sense. I know you want them to make sense, because you're a kid. But Rob isn't dying because it's a trade for Juliet. He saved Juliet when she was being held by . . . by Coach Gary. She would have died."

"Yes . . ."

"He's dying because of XP."

"So that's how you'll die."

With the same fingers I'd been using to hold her in a bruising grip, I pulled Angela close to me. "Angie, honey, look at me. I'm not dying. Maybe someday I'll die, and maybe it will be before you're grown up. But I hope not. Maybe there will be medicine . . ." I glanced at my mother, who nodded. "It will be very soon and help me get well. It could happen, Angela. It's not all death. I'm not sick now. Juliet's not sick now. She's getting better. She'll go home soon. If it were like the way Keely says, I would tell you."

Angela's eyes spilled over. Remarkably, then, she began to kick me, hard blows with her little soft-toed ballet flats.

"Shut up!" she said. "All you do is lie. You said Juliet was dead. You said she was a zombie angel."

Juliet appeared in the doorway, trailing her pole.

"Angela! Stop kicking Allie!"

Angela stopped.

"Angela, you have to forgive your sister. Same for you, Allie. She's scared," Juliet said. "She's *nine*. Wouldn't you be scared?" I thought about it; birth, rebirth, death, Christmas, and infinity crammed into a single corridor and a single week. *What did you do on your winter break, Angela?*

Juliet said, "Angie, come with me, okay? Ginny, my mom, is in my room and making you a sweater, and I think it's too big, because you're still pretty small. I don't think you grew a bit since I went away. It's grey and it's cable-knit."

Angela said clearly, "I don't want a goddamned sweater."

"What?" I said. "What did you say?"

"I said I don't want a fucking sweater."

"*What?*"

Juliet stepped between us, "But a sweater is better than nothing. And my mom's sweaters are better than most things. She makes them really long, so you can put a chain belt low, around your hips? Over leggings or a mini and leggings? And they are so soft. I mean, what's softer than alpaca? She shears her own alpaca. But you know that. You know our alpaca. You know our alpaca named Holly. And you know our alpaca named Soot. Do you like cable or plain?"

"Cable," Angela said. "I had one once. Duh. I was seven."

"Of course. Was that grey or black?"

"Grey."

"I still think this one will be too big."

"Except not. I grew an inch while you were gone. I gained seven pounds, Juliet. And you wear them long. You wear them down to here." She made a chopping motion at her mid-thigh.

"Well," Juliet said. "I don't know. Come and show me how long."

To my relief, Angela followed Juliet, who told Jackie and me to send Mrs. Staples our way when she arrived. I pushed my lounge close to Rob's bedside.

My mother sat in a chair, her computer open.

Rob's condition was slightly improved from rest and fluids. His breath was slow, but quiet. For the next five or six hours, his parents would be gone, picking up Rob's grandmother from Arizona, who normally came for a month in the summer. With a blanket rolled to provide some support for my neck, I fell asleep.

When I woke, I heard a voice calling, "Brownie! Get back here. Right now!"

It was a child's cry.

But it wasn't a child. It was Rob.

The skin of my face tightening and tingling, I sat up. Rob was wide-awake, too, and also sitting up in bed. "Brownie!" he called again. "Here."

In the dimness of the room, my mother looked straight at me. "This is all normal, sweetheart," she said. "He's hallucinating. He's not in any pain. Remember what I told you, it doesn't hurt." Bonnie had told me the same thing.

Brownie had been Rob's chocolate lab, a huge, sturdy, and loyal dog who'd died three years before when she, and Rob, were fourteen.

"You can talk to him," Jackie said. "I'm not sure he'll know it's you. But he'll hear you."

"Uh, what's she doing, Rob?" I said, softly.

Rob said, "She wants to go back in the water. See? She's like half fish. Crazy old dog."

"I see."

"Mom, you call her," Rob said. "Do the two-finger whistle!"

My mother shook her head. Rob was talking to me, not to her. I studied my mother's eyes. Calmly, tears forming, she nodded.

Using the heels of my hands to push my own tears away, I called softly, "Brownie, behave. You get over here. Right now!"

"Hah! She just kept on going, Mom! You're losing your touch."

What could I do? Rob was not breathing slowly or in a labored way. He was not asleep. He looked stronger than he had in weeks. If there was something I was supposed to do, Jackie would tell me. She had not stirred from her chair, only closed her laptop and set it on the ground. From studying her face, I intuited what she would want, if the dying boy in the bed was her dying girl. I knew what I should do.

Slowly, I said, "Should you run after her?"

"Oh, fine, Mom. Leave it to the man. I can catch up with her."

"Well, go ahead, then, if you're the big dog trainer. You're just standing there talking. I don't see you bringing that dog back."

"Mom, if Allie comes, make her stay here. I think Brownie scares her. Crazy old dog. Brownie!"

"I will, Rob. I'll make sure she stays here." I gulped, a gasp caught in my throat. But I recovered. "I think she's scared of Brownie. I guess we should have taught her not to be so rough."

Rob opened his arms wide. "Brownie! Get out of there! Don't you dare go in that swamp. You're going to be a slime ball. Wait for me!" Rob turned to me with a smile of blazing joy, then fell back on his heap of pillows.

When I reached out for his hand, his fingers tightened around mine.

"Go on, honey," I said. "I love you. I'll always love you."

In my hand, Rob's fingers began to cool. Jackie reached out and took Rob's other hand. Jackie stood, then tucked the blankets around his big shoulders as though he were a baby. In the dark, my mother and I sat, holding Rob's hands. I only reached up long enough to unhook the chain from my neck and slip that beautiful ring onto my hand.

After all, it was my eighteenth birthday.

I hope Brownie really was waiting for him. I hope that she leaped up on him, her paws almost touching his shoulders. And then, I hope they ran, Brownie weaving around Rob's knees as the sun spattered the water. Because the sun couldn't hurt either of them anymore.

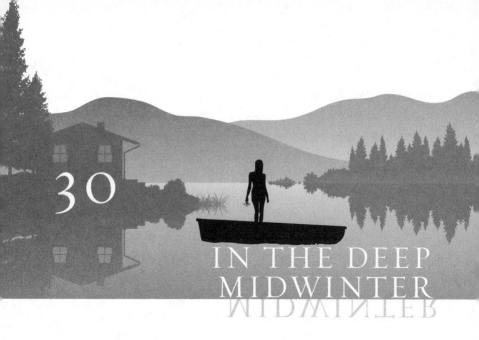

30

IN THE DEEP MIDWINTER

We said goodbye to Rob on a cold winter night.

It was all so familiar.

The casket was a plain, polished wooden box. Rob would have insisted on that. Thick-bladed machinery had hacked a deep square in the iron earth at Torch Mountain Cemetery. I remembered all the nights we'd spent pranking Daytimers there, pushing the guy who jilted Juliet into the new grave.

Only just over a year ago?

How many lifetimes?

We had all been so very young.

The pallbearers, wearing dark shirts and slacks, with white gloves, were Rob's cousin Victor, a Navy cadet at Annapolis, Mr. Sirocco, Bonnie, Gideon Brave Bear, Juliet, and me.

The service at St. Dunstan's of Canterbury had been excruciating: Rob's aunts, mother, and grandmother were perfect ladies, but even the long old-fashioned mantillas they wore couldn't conceal the deep lines on their faces. My mother used to say, "I can still look good; it just takes more sleep and more makeup." Mrs. Dorn's careful makeup made smudges under her eyes where she had cried and tried to wipe away the marks. Why, I thought briefly, didn't she use waterproof? Then, immediately, I could not imagine her walking into Waldermann's and asking for the right kind of makeup for her only child's funeral.

The church was beautiful, candlelit at the fall of evening, the pews draped with big red-velvet bows, as they would have been for a wedding. All the flowers were pots of holly, Christmas wreathes, or big tubs of red and white poinsettias.

The Dorns were Episcopalian, but I'd never thought about that much until now. After the blessings and some Bible passages, the priest spoke. "Rob sometimes came to our Saturday night services, especially in the winter. Recently, he'd come to talk to me on several occasions. Every one of us has questions about death and what life has meant. This was difficult for me because the usual rules don't apply. I still don't understand why a young man who embodies so much good would try so hard to make the best of what he had and still lose his life so young," the priest said. "I do know this. Rob was a child, still. But he also was a man. In St. John, chapter fifteen, verse thirteen, it says, in the Anglican tradition I came from, 'Greater love hath no man more than this, that a man lay down his life for his friends.'"

The priest put a hand over his eyes and seemed to gather his strength. "Rob Dorn might have gone on living comfortably at least for a short time longer. But he laid down his life for a friend." The priest paused and seemed to summon strength. "We all know evil exists in the world. Rob faced evil to save his friend, Juliet Sirocco, from a torment that was like the trials of the biblical Job. But the Bible says, in Luke, 'Fear not them who can kill the body,' because that is all that they can do. Even the evil can kill the body, but they cannot kill the spirit. So Rob's spirit lives on, in everyone whose life he touched and renewed, in the good he did, because that can never die."

People sang then. Someone had picked a song that everyone knew, a song that Mrs. Dorn sang to Rob when he was a baby, "You Are My Sunshine," which was awful, because someone had taken her sunshine away.

The last person who stood and spoke was Juliet's dad, Tommy Sirocco. "Dennis and Elizabeth," he said. "Dennis. And Elizabeth." Tommy coughed and began again. "I want to tell you, Dennis. And Elizabeth."

Then, he just bent forward with his hands on the podium, his big shoulders shaking as though he were nodding his head in the rhythm of a song only he could hear. He had to sit back down without saying anything. What he wanted to say, we already knew. He wanted to thank the Dorns for raising a hero.

There were only two things left, one more piece of ritual: the quiet finality of the cemetery. I thought, as I got ready to walk outside, how could I leave my Rob, whose body I had known and loved, alone in the cold? It was just a place, after all, and it wasn't really going to be Rob. Still, everything I ever knew of Rob on this Earth was going to be there. The line of cars made its way up the steep road. In the black mourner's car, I sat with my mother, my sister, and Gina, as well as Juliet and her parents.

The funeral director had set up a line of small torches along the road, each enclosed in a glass globe. At the grave site, there were four big torches, muted lights set well away from the place that had been cleared of snow, where there was a rough piece of canvas and several rows of folding chairs, each with a blanket on the seat.

In the car, Juliet and I put on our dark wool coats and white gloves. Unlike military pallbearers, we had been taught at Bergey's Funeral Services to carry the casket three on each side, each using one hand, walking straight forward. At military funerals, Rob's cousin had told us, the soldiers carried the fallen one with the coffin at shoulder height. Victor had that same frightening, flushed look of responsibility and grim excitement that was on Mr. Dorn's own face. *This isn't real to him quite yet,* I realized.

Bonnie appeared at my elbow with a smile that combined pity and encouragement. Just a few more steps, she seemed to say, pulling on her own gloves.

I straightened up and waited for Mr. Bergey to open the back of the hearse.

There, just a little farther up the hill, was the grave of my friend, Nicola Burns. Next to her tombstone were those of Nicola's mother, and Mr. Ackerman, our favorite tutor, who had XP and committed suicide two years before. And Nicola had died just . . . a year ago and a little bit. A spring and a fall and a winter, and now another winter. A year, and change. It wasn't possible that all this could have fit into such a slender space of time, a few leaves of a calendar, just two of my little moleskin journals.

"We're ready now," said Mr. Bergey.

The six of us grasped the brass handles.

I thought, *I am carrying you, my dearest love.*

After we set the casket down on a kind of metal gurney, Mr. Bergey turned one of the lights up slightly. The soft pine of the box glowed against the fresh snow, on a big woolen blanket of dark blue with stars embroidered on it, which Ginny Sirocco had sewn to replace the usual roll of fake grass. The priest nodded to me.

For the second time in three months I'd been asked to read a poem to commemorate my best friend. How does that happen in such a short space in one's life? But now the body of my friend, my playmate, the only man I would ever love, was here, truly here, in this box. And instead, Juliet— my other best friend, my playmate, my confidante, the girl I'd believed lost to me forever—stood so close to me I could hear the soft, repeated catch in her breathing. Although she was still terribly thin, her cheeks had filled out; the sores that roughened the corners of her mouth had closed; and her short hair curled clean and soft.

She stood Juliet-straight, the abrupt bones of her spine nearly like the wings of the angel zombie. She stood at my back.

I could hear her crying. I realized that I could count on one hand the times I'd heard Juliet cry. Her mother Ginny leaned forward and handed Juliet one of Tommy's big hand- kerchiefs. At that moment, I saw something else: Juliet's immense joy and wonder at being here, despite everything. Once again she was under her mother and her father's wing, and with me. She was the living embodiment of survivor guilt at its piercing pinnacle. Juliet was tough, but not tough enough for this.

Jackie had helped me find the poem. She remembered hearing it read at a funeral in a favorite movie. Jackie thought that the poet, A. E. Housman, must have known a boy like that, a boy who never gave less than his best, like Rob, and then there was a war, and Housman had written "To an Athlete Dying Young." I began to read it.

The time you won your town the race
We chaired you through the market-place;
Man and boy stood cheering by,
And home we brought you shoulder-high.

I thought of big, boisterous Rob bouldering like an oversized marsupial from handle to handle along the walls and ceilings in his home gym. Rob, ripped in every muscle group, balanced shirtless at the pier on a summer night, in the handstand he could hold forever. Rob, a forward sinking three-pointers for hours before no cheering crowd on the dark half-court in his backyard, the mountaineer who never got to dance his triumph in the sunlight.

To-day, the road all runners come,
Shoulder-high we bring you home,
And set you at your threshold down,
Townsman of a stiller town.

Smart lad, to slip betimes away
From fields where glory does not stay,
And early though the laurel grows
It withers quicker than the rose.

The flat bronze marker already set against a young birch tree had no dates. It read only:

ROBERT ALEXANDER DORN
BEST SON, BEST FRIEND

I folded the paper.
Mr. Dorn kissed my cheek. I hugged him. I didn't dare

go near Mrs. Dorn; it was as natural to shy from the white-hot power of a mother's grief as it was to shun a wild horse. Turning away, I stood beside Juliet while the priest said his last words. He invited the group to join the Dorn's for a small dinner in a private room at the Timbers Restaurant at Torch Mountain. The other restaurant Rob loved was closed. Passing the marquee at Gitchee, we noticed that where it usually read, 2 LGE, 2 TOPPINGS, $5, tonight read: MISS U ROB. Gid's wife stood in the small crowd, hugely pregnant. Maybe Gid would have his son.

At the last moment, Mrs. Dorn laid the blue blanket over the casket and tucked in the edges, in a way I recognized from the hundreds of times I'd seen my mother do that at Angela's bedside . . . and my own.

Everyone walked away, except for two people who stayed behind.

We were the *tres compadres*.

31

THE LOVE YOU MAKE

THE LOVE YOU MAKE

Juliet knew I might want to spend a few moments there alone, so, being Juliet, she stayed. If I could feel even a flicker of amusement, it was to recognize that Juliet's concept of personal space always included her in it.

She would drive me home. Halfway down the hill, her own car was parked on Methodist Avenue. Torch Mountain Home Cemetery had a quaint way of making sure birds of a feather slept together on the same branch.

Juliet said, "How are you?"

"I wouldn't know."

"It's cold, but not as cold as it was yesterday. That's good. The wind has stopped," Juliet said. "The stars are out."

"You sound like someone in an old play." She took my arm and I glanced up, thinking, as a crescent moon appeared, of the gigantic star-spattered window above Rob's bed.

In five days, he would have been eighteen years old.

Then, out of the corner of my eye, some distance away, I suddenly caught a glimpse of something unexplainable.

There was old Dr. Simon Tabor standing next to Dr. Andrew.

Dr. Andrew was holding the old man's arm as Dr. Simon Tabor used an evergreen bough to dust the fine frosting of snow away from identical polished marble bricks. Two matching headstones, etched in silver, and one smaller, black marble.

It was not just unexplainable, but impossible. Perhaps they'd stood, unnoticed, at the back of the crowd, to pay their respects to Rob. Now they were tending their own family graves. The new one was Garrett Tabor's. For a moment, I wanted to cry out: How dare fate let him lie so close to my beloved? I had to remind myself again. Neither one of them, small and evil or great and good, was really there. But I wouldn't let the doctor walk away without paying their respects—to me. And to Juliet. If they would mourn Garrett Tabor, they had to acknowledge what he was.

On impulse, with Juliet keeping pace, I walked over to where the two men stood. Then I stopped.

I could see Dr. Andrew's face. Always handsome, he was now haggard. He was a good man, and you could see how grief—over Rob and Dr. Stephen, over his nephew, and, probably, his own reputation, on the eve of his greatest advance in battling XP—had carved deep grooves in his skin. No longer did he look younger than most guys his age. He looked tired and beaten-up, as though something had been punched out of him.

I nearly turned away, but he had seen me.

"Oh, Allie. Dear Allie. Oh, Juliet," said Dr. Andrew. "I don't know what to say. Juliet, you're the one star in all this blackness. There's nothing I can say that can express how I feel. The shame is overpowering. The fear of what might prove to be true."

"It's not what might be true," Juliet said softly. "It's all true, Dr. Andrew. There's no doubt."

"I know," he said miserably.

Glancing at Juliet, I said, "Hello, Dr. Simon."

"Our family is so sorry for this loss, Allie," Dr. Simon said. "We're sorry for the role someone in our family played in this loss."

Dr. Andrew followed Dr. Simon's sweeping hand down to the two identical silver headstones. Dr. Andrew cleared his throat. "This is my sister-in-law, Stephen's wife, Merry Whitcomb Green, and their daughter, Rachel. Rachel died at just three years old. They died in an automobile crash. Garrett and Grant and their sister Rebecca survived, and we often wonder . . . it was twenty years ago now. There was no cell phone capability up here. It was Christmas Eve. Remember, Pop? Stephen knew Merry was gone the moment he looked at her. Her head was so badly injured from the roof column of the car. No one could have survived that."

Dr. Simon nodded. His eyes were rheumy. "Such a steadfast woman. That was how I thought of her. Steadfast. She was very pretty, and a very good dancer, but she never lost sight of the fact that her first mission was to those children. A wonderful mother. Stephen was lost without her."

"So Stephen hitchhiked. He carried Rebecca, and Grant and he hitched a ride with a logger," Dr. Andrew continued, nodding at us. "He got Grant and Rebecca to the emergency room. Then he turned back. Rachel was crying, but she was in the proper restraints. Stephen told . . . his son . . . my nephew, Garrett, not to move her . . ."

"He got back and she was dead," Simon Tabor said. "Not a mark on her anywhere. They never determined the cause of death."

"Stephen was haunted by that. He thought he should have known. I think it was one of the reasons that he became a coroner." Dr. Andrew shrugged, and seemed to shrink in his dark coat. He said, "Allie. Stephen. My brother . . ."

I nodded, moved aside as old Simon Tabor pulled away from Andrew and began to march toward their car. For some reason, the night felt colder. The wind was finally bucking up. Simon walked straight and did not flinch from the gusts, his level shoulders a testament to a life of mental puzzling and physical exertion. Then, as if to himself, the old man said, "She wouldn't have lived very long, in any case. Those children didn't have a chance back then, not even as much as these young ladies here."

Dr. Andrew said, "Who do you mean, Pop?"

"You know, the kids we treat."

"What do you mean?"

"Xeroderma Pigmentosum, Andrew. Stephen's girl had XP. Rachel. The only one of the four who did."

"Little Rachel. Stephen's younger daughter. You're saying she had XP." You see people do this in movies, but Dr. Andrew literally took a step back and seemed to stagger in his sensible, waffle-soled, black dress boots. He whispered, "What are you saying?"

"Andrew, this was why I changed my research focus from cystic fibrosis. I had grown up with a boy, our next-door neighbor in Chicago, a truly brave lad. On spring nights, I would hear him coughing, his parents percussing his back. That horrible, wet sound. Danny . . . Danny Angstrom. That's right. The parents had three healthy children, just the way that Stephen and Merry did. Then came Danny. Just like this little girl . . ."

"Rachel was a normal, healthy baby, Pop. I watched her grow. After they came up here, I saw her all the time."

"You were in London. You saw her a few times."

"Right, yes. Of course."

"Stephen knew, of course.

"But Father, you told us that the reason that you changed your focus to XP was the complexities of the disease and its genetic variation . . ."

"Well that goes without saying, that it was compelling," Dr. Simon Tabor said, seeming to lose interest. Touching the brim of his wool hat to us, he motioned to Andrew to open the car doors. Andrew pressed the button and the Mercedes' big lights blinked. The horn gave a muted bleat.

But Dr. Andrew didn't move.

"Pop!" Dr. Andrew cried. "My son has two children! My own three children were never tested for XP. They would have needed to be tested when they were children. And my grandchildren could have been tested before birth."

The old man muttered, "Your children are fine. So are your grandsons. Those boys are just fine."

"They should have had testing in the first trimester. What were you thinking? If this is true . . . then, for three generations, you orphaned me from my own family's genetic destiny. Pop! Listen to me!" Quieter, Dr. Andrew said, "You didn't care, did you? It would have been . . . compelling. You're like him."

We didn't have to ask whom he meant.

The old man opened the passenger door of the silver Mercedes. He muttered something Juliet and I could barely hear—something about a family's privacy and his concern being for Stephen's family and their grief. He closed the door with a sharp clap. Dr. Andrew stood there with us. He clutched the sides of his head. I almost reached out for him. Juliet held on. Her wrist was half the width of mine, and her grip was like her chains, nothing I could have broken, with all my strength.

"All this with Garrett, and now . . . I'm afraid I don't know what my father is talking about. I almost hope that he's experiencing dementia. You don't understand what this would mean."

"Oh, we do," Juliet said. "We really do."

"My children, and their children . . ."

"They could have been us."

"Yes, but it's not as though . . . when you put it that way, it sounds terrible," Dr. Andrew said. "No one would choose for a child to have XP."

"Juliet, he's right," I said, desperately sorry for this man, deluded in the safety of his own empire, tricked by close-up magic.

"I'm sorry, of course. But still, welcome to our world, Dr. Andrew," said Juliet. "Family secrets are a bad business. In your family, bad secrets are tradition."

In the muted light from the electric torches, Dr. Andrew's eyes were wide and limpid as a deer's. We knew that the Bergeys, father and sons, were close by. We knew that when the real work of burial could begin, they would steal in, like ghosts, and set up some big industrial lights. Many times, the real grave was filled at night, out of the sight of people who could not bear the sight. But the Bergeys were trained, as all people in this business are trained, in patience. There were a few businesses like funeral homes.

Bakeries. Fishing.

If no one in the family did it before you, why would anyone ever choose to do it?

Medicine was sometimes this way, too, a legacy of pain and achievement. Dr. Andrew said, "Please. Forgive me, Juliet. I didn't know."

"We forgive you," Juliet said. Her grip on my arm loosened—now a touch, tender, like a link. "You're of them but not like them. You're a good person, Dr. Andrew." The terrible knowledge of what might have happened on that lonely road on a Christmas Eve twenty years ago, of who might have been Garrett Tabor's first and tiniest victim swung between Dr. Andrew and us, like a dark pendulum. "It's time to go now, Allie."

I said, "I know."

As we started down the hill, I glanced back at the star-covered blanket over Rob's casket, and I saw that Dr. Andrew had continued to walk away from us, up high, to the hilltop, where he stood silhouetted against the bright night. We couldn't see his face. But his hands were lifted, as though he were reaching for something.

Juliet and I made our way, sticking close together, careful not to slip in the places before the snow gave way to the hardpack road. Suddenly, she said, "I'm going to go to college, too, Bear. I want to be like Bonnie. I want to be FBI."

"I don't know if that's possible."

"Let's pretend it is, until we know it isn't," Juliet said. "None of this was possible."

I was ravenous, my hunger as rude and demanding as life itself, but I did not want to go to the Timbers. Juliet and I would ride through the night, and find our own place.

Behind us was the past. We would always belong to it. It was beloved, intransigent, impenetrable, coils of darkness and rings of light. The past was closer to us than what lay ahead. Still, we had to leave it. We had to look away.

Just then, a banner of fireworks shot out above the ridge at Torch Mountain, fragmenting wheels and fonts of blue and red and gold. What was it? Not New Year's Eve. Perhaps a wedding. Yes. Fireworks often accompanied a winter wedding. I touched the ring on my hand.

Then Juliet and I held hands and began to run, as if to try to catch up, our faces polished by the distant sliver of light. I was eighteen. It was a new year.

And technically, it was already morning.

ACKNOWLEDGMENTS

ACKNOWLEDGMENTS

This is a work of fiction, and while I did my best, all the errors in it are entirely mine. Thanks are due to Bonnie Sommers-Olsen, medical counselor and friend, to Dr. Gay, expert in everything, to authors Mitchell Wieland and Wiley Cash, and especially Richard Adams Carey, who taught me more than I knew that I didn't know. Gratitude is owed to The Corporation of Yaddo, where I wrote the final pages of this book in the fall of 2012. Thanks to Karen Cooper, founder and publisher of Merit Press, for her support of my need to try to be a great writing editor. Thanks to my colleague Meredith O'Hayre for her patience with my many ineptitudes and Monday-morning humor. Great gratitude goes also to Soho's Daniel Ehrenhaft, for believing in this strange and out-of-character story, to Jane Gelfman, for twenty-seven years agent and best friend, to Pamela, to Jean, to Gemma, to Carol, to Ann, to Bobby, my bro, to Tom, Kathy, Greg, Susan, and Lisa, who occupy the permanent suite in my heart, and to those who own the land—Rob, Dan, Martin, Francie, Merit, Mia, Will, Marta, and Atticus.